MORE THAN A HORSE

BY C. S. ADLER

CLARION BOOKS
NEW YORK

My thanks to Jeanne Place for reading this book to check my horse lore and lingo.

Thanks to Ann Long who was kind enough to read the manuscript for correctness on the therapeutic riding program.

Much appreciation to Fern Pivar and her daughter Stephanie who welcomed me into their home and taught me a lot, and not only about the therapeutic riding program.

Clarion Books
a Houghton Mifflin Company imprint
215 Park Avenue South, New York, NY 10003
Text copyright © 1997 by C. S. Adler
The text for this book was set in 12/15-point Galliard.

For information about this and other Houghton Mifflin trade and
reference books and multimedia products, visit The Bookstore at
Houghton Mifflin on the World Wide Web at
(http://www.hmco.com/trade/).

Printed in the USA

Library of Congress Cataloging-in-Publication Data

Adler, C. S. (Carole S.)
More than a horse / by C. S. Adler.
p.   cm.
Summary: When her mother takes a job on a guest ranch in Arizona,
twelve-year-old Leeann hopes to be able to ride whenever she wants,
but it takes her own perseverance and the help of new friends,
including the mother of a handicapped child,
to win over the ranch's crusty wrangler.
ISBN 0-395-79769-1
[1. Horses—Fiction.   2. Friendship—Fiction.
3. Dude ranches—Fiction.   4. Arizona—Fiction.]   I. Title.
PZ7.A26145Mo   1997
[Fic]—dc20   96-42175
CIP
AC

BP 10 9 8 7 6 5 4 3 2 1

For Jeanne Place
and Helga and Mervyn Prichard
whose friendship has brightened my life.

CHAPTER 1 ----------------

"We're going to be lucky this time," Rose said. "I can feel it." Her round face glowed with hope as she drove west toward her new job, even though the Arizona sunshine glared fiercely along the empty road.

Leeann had always enjoyed her mother's optimism and wished she had more of it. Now she made herself say deliberately, "It'll be great to ride whenever I want."

"Good enough to make up for not getting that horse Big John promised you?" Rose asked.

Leeann swallowed hard. "Almost," she said. She even managed a smile when Rose's eyes turned from the road long enough to read her face. The current of affection flowing between them energized them both. Maybe they would be lucky this time, Leeann told herself. Why not? If anyone deserved to be lucky, it was Rose who tried so hard and loved so much.

Ahead of their station wagon, the mountains lay like sleeping dinosaurs against the stainless blue sky.

1

Leeann had never seen such mountains. They weren't green like the ones in North Carolina where she'd been born, but brown and jagged. The flat desert through which Leeann and Rose were driving was speckled with scraggly little bushes and cactuses. A tall cactus, the kind that the man at the gas station had called saguaro, stuck up like a huge green thumb against Leeann's first view of the ranch. Thumbs up, right on, welcome—she got the message and laughed when her mother's childhood friend Hanna came lumbering toward them from the porch. Arms flung wide, Hanna was yelling, "Welcome to Lost River Ranch!"

Rose stepped out of the car and the two women hugged each other hard.

"See, I told you your old wagon would hold up," Hanna concluded triumphantly.

Rose patted the nearest dented fender and said, "The poor thing deserves a medal. These western highways go on forever. And how it got us over the mountains I'll never know. But anyway, we're here."

Leeann returned Hanna's embrace warmly when it was her turn to be hugged, even though she only knew Hanna from a couple of visits. The most recent one had been two years ago when Leeann was ten. That had been before Big John had blown through their lives.

"So, I hear you're quite the horsewoman," Hanna said. The cast on her right arm whacked Leeann clumsily on the back. "Sorry," Hanna said.

"I keep forgetting I'm packaged in plaster." Her eyes were kind in a weathered face that looked years older than Rose's although they were both only in their late thirties.

"I haven't had a chance to ride much," Leeann said, "so I don't know how good a horsewoman I am. But I love horses."

"Too bad that bum your mother fell for took off before he gave you the horse he promised you," Hanna said.

Leeann's eyes went to her mother for help. Rose had warned that Hanna could be blunt. Goodhearted but forthright, was how Mother had put it.

"Big John meant well," Rose said calmly. "He just got carried away with his own ideas."

"Leaving you to pay his debts." Hanna pointed at Rose and said, "She always believes the best of people. I hope you're tougher." She studied Leeann for a minute. Then she said, "You look like your daddy. He was long and lanky and blond. But you got your mother's eyes."

"Thanks," Leeann said. She thought Rose was beautiful and wished she had her mother's ruddy cheeks and red-gold hair.

"Well, there's plenty of horses here," Hanna said. "But you may have to muck out a few stalls and clean a few hooves before Amos lets you ride any. He's our head wrangler, and he's got more work than he and the two that work under him can handle."

Even with her broken arm, which was the reason Rose had been hired to help Hanna do the cooking for the guest ranch, Hanna insisted on helping them unload the station wagon. It was stuffed up to and on top of its roof with all their remaining belongings, including the good dishes and silverware Rose had inherited from her mother. To cover Big John's debts, Rose had sold off the business she'd struggled so hard to build, but she'd hung onto her family treasures.

They each took what they could carry, and Hanna guided them to a cabin amidst a jumble of outbuildings behind the main house. Leeann had understood they were coming to a working guest ranch, not a luxury resort, but she was taken aback by the size of the one-bedroom cabin she and Rose had been assigned. "Rustic" was how Hanna had described it over the phone. Inside, the walls were raw wood and there didn't seem to be any storage space except for one small closet and a few shelves over the hot plate that would serve as their "kitchen" area.

"We could stow Grandma's dishes under the bed," Leeann said quickly when she saw her mother's bright cheeks fade in chagrin.

"It's small," Hanna said. "I told you it would be, but at least it's free with the job. You two don't mind sharing a bed, do you?"

Rose shook her head distractedly. Even in their modest house in North Carolina, she and Leeann had each had her own bedroom. And in the house Big John had begun building for them there would have been five bedrooms and bathrooms galore.

"We won't be spending much time indoors here anyway," Leeann said. She and Rose had agreed on their long drive to this south central portion of Arizona that they were on an adventure and they were going to enjoy it no matter what.

"Maybe *you'll* be outdoors, but your mother will be spending her days in the ranch house's kitchen," Hanna said. "That's where you'll find her until the last guest leaves in May and the Holdens close up for the summer."

"We'll be fine," Rose said. The old glow was back in her cheeks, and the dark amber of her hair and eyes reflected it. Leeann was buoyed up as always by her mother's unfailing good nature. Never mind how cramped this cabin was. Never mind that Rose wasn't trained as a cook. This was a new beginning, "a place they could both grow in" as Rose had put it.

Through the flyspecked kitchen window, Leeann saw horses in a field. "Do those belong to the ranch?" she asked Hanna.

"Far as the eye can see, everything's part of Lost River Ranch. Saturday is turnover day when the old guests leave and new ones arrive. There's no trail rides and the horses get turned out to pasture. Not that there's much there for them besides dry prickery stuff. This is the Sonoran desert, and what grows best is brittle bush and mesquite, cactus and creosote bushes."

"Okay if I go out and say hi to a horse or two?" Leeann asked.

"Go ahead," Hanna said. "Your mother and I need time for a real heart-to-heart chat. Better take a jug of water with you though. We don't go anywhere without water. It's real dry after the January rains." Hanna gestured at the empty plastic bottles lined up near the freestanding kitchen sink. "Oh, say, where's my head. If you're hungry, you'd best come out to the kitchen first."

"No, thanks. We stopped for lunch," Leeann said. Lunch had been three hours ago, and she *was* hungry, but she was too eager to get to the horses to want to stop and eat.

"Just don't tangle with any rattlesnakes or scorpions, Leeann," Rose said, but she was smiling.

Leeann got a pungent whiff of horse manure and sweated leather as she walked past the barn. The ramada, the long shady porch that ran along the front of the main house, was full of suitcases and guests waiting for transportation. The biggest corral, to one side of the main ranch house, was empty. Leeann walked past it toward the barbed wire fence, which was held up every so often by crooked posts. They marched up hill and down as far as she could see. Behind them was the silent menagerie of mountains. Gorgeous, Leeann thought. Better than she'd dreamed.

She slipped between the strands of barbed wire and approached a knobby-kneed horse munching on dry grass. It moved off to get away from her, but a small bay turned its head her way, then ambled toward her.

"My first friend," she whispered to the bay as she stroked its neck. A saddle sore marred its smooth hide. Its soft muzzle poked at her as if it were looking for a treat. When it didn't find any, it lost interest and sauntered off.

Leeann kept walking through the desert scrub toward sandstone cliffs that seemed closer than they probably were. Up a rise she saw a trail cobbled with hoofprints as if it were well used by riders. And there past a pile of truck-sized boulders stood a handsome mahogany-colored horse with black tail and mane. Leeann caught her breath at the way the animal's muscular beauty stood out against the dreamy blue of the sky. She climbed the hill to get to him, but he was watching her, and when she got close, he pawed the earth and snorted in a threatening way. The flare of his nostrils and the arrogant lift of his head made her hesitate. Maybe this one wasn't friendly. But she wasn't afraid of horses. Big as they were, she trusted in their good nature. Slowly she continued walking, talking to the animal as she got closer.

"Hi, fella. It's just me, Leeann. I'm coming to say hello."

The horse whinnied. Some tension in his stance warned her before the voice did.

"Hey, you! Get away from that stallion." A man on horseback came riding at her. His long gray hair was tied back in a ponytail and he wore his cowboy hat so low it seemed hung up on his thick gray eyebrows. "What are you doing? You're on private property." The man sounded angry and his eyebrows bristled at her.

"I'm not doing anything wrong," she said. "I was just making friends with the horses."

"What you're making is trouble."

"No, really," she said. "I'm Leeann Peters. My mother's the new cook. And I—"

"No matter. I'm Amos, the head wrangler here. Now get out of this field and don't let me catch you pestering a horse again without permission."

He turned his horse as smoothly as if it were an extension of his legs, and rode off without looking back. His confidence in her obedience impressed Leeann as much as his fierceness. But she wasn't worried. She trusted that Hanna would straighten him out.

Later, when Hanna introduced Leeann to Amos formally after dinner and mentioned how much Leeann loved horses and that she would be willing to work with them for free, it didn't help. Amos glowered at her and walked off quickly into the dark.

"He was mad because you could have gotten

8

hurt. That horse was Darth Vader, the stud. He's dangerous, and you were challenging him on his territory," Hanna explained.

"You said she'd have a chance to ride, Hanna," Rose said.

"She will if she can get on Amos's good side," Hanna said. "He's a grouch, and unfortunately what he decides about the horses goes." Her voice poured sympathy thick as syrup as she added, "Better give Amos time to cool off before you try winning him over, Leeann."

"How much time?" Leeann asked.

"I guess till he stops glaring when he sees you." Hanna laughed as if that were funny.

Leeann didn't think it was. If she couldn't ride, there was nothing here to console her for not getting a horse of her own. Nothing to keep her from feeling like a loose stone rattling around the world owning nothing, belonging nowhere. She stared into the darkness of the unknown night and was struck by how lonely it seemed.

CHAPTER 2 ————————————————

While she hung about the ranch that weekend waiting for Amos to relent, Leeann got more and more anxious about how the other part of her life here in Arizona would be. School. Monday she'd have to start out in the middle of seventh grade in a class where she didn't know anyone and where they might be well-launched into unfamiliar subjects. But she'd always been a pretty good student. What worried her most was how she'd fit in socially.

She'd been so comfortable back in Charlotte, North Carolina, even though her two closest friends had moved away in sixth grade. Since kindergarten, she'd been an accepted member of her class, not a star but accepted, at least until Big John's scams had turned some of her schoolmates against her.

The first shock had been an anonymous note. "Your mother married a crook, and where do you come off living in that big house he ripped people off to pay for?" Then the girls Leeann had been sitting with at lunch didn't leave a place for her at their table anymore. She had hidden her hurt, even when someone threw a wet clay ball that hit the back of her best white sweater, but the hostility devastated her. She had lost confidence that she was welcome, even among boys and girls who had nothing to hold against her.

Before Big John's business ventures fell apart, he had promised so much. "My honey girls," he had called Rose and Leeann, and he'd put his strong arms around them and told them they'd never have to pinch pennies again. "And you know what, Leeann?" he'd said. "You're going to get a horse of your own." Like her mother and the people in town whose life savings he'd taken, Leeann hadn't doubted genial, dynamic Big John—not for a minute.

When Big John disappeared from their lives, he'd left Rose liable for the loans she'd cosigned. She had sold her upholstery business, paid off their creditors, and talked about getting a job in an office. Leeann knew how bad her mother was at that kind of work. Ever since she'd brought home an A in math when she was ten, she'd been keeping Rose's checkbook for her and reminding her of when the insurance bills were due and the car needed inspecting.

"Frankly, I'd be just as glad to leave town and start somewhere new," Rose had said when they were packing to move out of the big house. Then Hanna had broken her wrist and called to ask if Rose thought she'd like to try out another career.

"A cook? Rose, you don't know anything about cooking," Leeann had said.

"Thanks a lot. Just because I let the Thanksgiving turkey stay in the oven too long . . ."

"No, I mean," Leeann had corrected herself, "I know you can do anything with your hands, but cooking for a lot of people—"

"I can learn. The thing is, Leeann, this is a dude ranch and there'll be horses for you to ride. You'd like that, wouldn't you?"

"Oh, Mama!" And Leeann had hugged Rose and been grateful.

"Keep busy," Rose always advised whenever she caught Leeann brooding about something. So that Sunday, her first weekend on the ranch, Leeann got to work. After breakfast she cleaned the cabin with Hanna's vacuum, and then she scrubbed the worn linoleum of the closet-sized kitchen and washed out the tiny refrigerator with baking soda. She worked on the rust-stained metal shower in the cramped bathroom and rubbed ammonia-soaked rags over the windows until most of the flyspecks and spider webs were gone.

When the cabin was as clean as she could get it, Leeann resettled the stacks of boxes that held all her mother's and her belongings. Finally there was nothing she could see to do, so she went to the corral fence and leaned on it to watch.

The ranch owner, Mr. Holden, to whom Leeann had been introduced briefly, was busy matching horses to guests. Helping him were Amos and his two wranglers—a cross-eyed scarecrow of a boy named Robuck and a silent, thickset middle-aged man named Hank. Standing next to a guest who had to weigh more than two hundred pounds, the elegantly slim Mr. Holden said cheerfully, "Amos, this gentleman's an experienced rider. He needs a horse with some spirit. Think Ramses would suit him?"

Amos nodded and brought out a large black horse that looked strong enough to handle any rider. "Don't rein him in too tight now," Mr. Holden advised the guest. "He'll fight you on a tight rein."

Meanwhile Amos was listening to a teenage girl describe her riding experience. Before she'd finished detailing the last lessons she'd had, he muttered something to Robuck, who went off to saddle up a lively looking pinto.

Hank brought out a dappled gray mare for a young woman whose boots and riding pants had the well-worn look of an experienced rider. Leeann watched enviously as the young woman swung gracefully into the saddle and directed Hank to shorten a stirrup for her. When Amos led off the first group of trail riders, Robuck took up the tail end position.

Mr. Holden was by then instructing five beginners who seemed to be the parents and three children of one family. After he'd taught them how to handle the reins, he advised them to sit in the saddle with their heels down. "You slide forward on the saddle to help the horse going uphill and slide back on the way down," he said.

Leeann watched patiently, but neither Hank nor Mr. Holden took notice of her. Finally, the beginners were led off for a ride by Hank, and Leeann had only the horses left behind in the corral for company. A heaviness settled on her, as if the broken promises of her life were weighing her down.

Sunday passed and Amos didn't relent. Leeann stared longingly at the horses. Much as she enjoyed watching them, it was tormenting to be so close and not even be allowed to touch one, much less to ride.

Monday Leeann put on her best jeans to go to the new school. She wore her long tawny hair loose to insure that, despite her thinness and the dark eyebrows that made her face appear stern, she wouldn't be mistaken for a boy. For the hundredth time she regretted that her hair wasn't the russet of a maple leaf like her mother's and that her skin didn't glow like Rose's. Her mother always told her to be glad she'd inherited her dead father's leanness and didn't have to worry about excess weight the way Rose did, but Leeann still felt gypped in the gene department.

Let there be a nice girl on the lookout for a friend in my class, she prayed silently.

The school was a low, sand-colored block building. It rambled through a bare, brownish-gray field studded with rocks. Dry brown hills were sketched against the sky behind it. Leeann had said she didn't need Rose to escort her the first day, but she was glad her mother had insisted.

"You may look sixteen, but you're only twelve," Rose had said, "Also, I want to see what this place is like myself."

The halls were light and full of student artwork. The classrooms were quiet and full of students bent over desks. "It *looks* fine," Rose said before she left.

"Fine," Leeann echoed reassuringly.

The classroom she was assigned to struck her as disorganized. The desks were clumped together haphazardly, and students seemed to be roving about at will, talking too loudly. The young teacher, Ms. Morabita, had black hair fixed in elaborate rolls and whorls, with a pencil stuck in it and dangly earrings hanging below it.

"We're just starting our initiative projects, Leeann," Ms. Morabita said. Her hands fidgeted and her eyes roved the room anxiously. "You fill out this form about your special likes, and I'll attach you to the right group. Okay?"

Leeann studied the form. Name your three favorite things in order of preference. Name your three favorite activities in order of preference. Name the three things you're best at. Leeann kept jotting down answers and scratching them out for fear they wouldn't leave a good impression of her. Half an hour later when she was done, her lists read:

15

Three favorite things are my mother, horses, nature. Three favorite activities are horseback riding, photography, sleeping. Three things I'm good at are math, working, organizing things.

She handed the list to the teacher, who smiled when she read it.

"Oh, good, this'll be easy. I'll just put you with Joy Childs's group. Their project is horses." Ms. Morabita fluttered her hands toward a clutch of desks in the corner of the room where two girls were sitting with two boys perched on desks near them.

Leeann didn't move.

Ms. Morabita asked, "Want me to introduce you?"

"Please," Leeann said. Her stomach clenched anxiously as she followed the teacher through the chattering students to the farthest corner. The groups didn't appear to be accomplishing much. Leeann liked orderly learning. She liked to know what the teacher expected so that she could complete a task and take satisfaction from doing it well. Here, she wouldn't even be able to tell what doing it well required. She was so nervous that she barely smiled when the teacher introduced her to the group.

"This is Leeann, and she likes horses, so I'm putting her with you guys. Okay?" Ms. Morabita said.

"Oh, sure. We could use some new blood," said a pretty girl with a cloud of long blond curly hair. She

16

smiled at Leeann. "I'm Joy, and this is Kristen, and Zach and Alan. We've been together since first grade, which means none of us can come up with an idea the rest of us haven't heard before, so we're stuck. What do you think we could do about horses?"

"I don't know," Leeann said, choking up at this new test.

"I'll leave you kids to it," Ms. Morabita said. She hurried toward a group who were yelling at each other.

"Well," Joy said, "my idea's to take a horse from the time it's born through its life. Kristen wants to do horses in general, and the boys want just working horses. What do you think?"

To Leeann's relief, an idea popped into her head. "How about doing horse personalities," she said. "Like the stories of individual horses and what's happened to them in their lives? Like horse portraits?"

Kristen, a small earnest-faced girl, neat as a black capped chickadee, said, "Horse portraits! I like that. Then you could do one horse from birth on, Joy, and the boys could pick working horses for their portraits."

"Do you own a horse, Leeann?" Joy asked.

"No. I was supposed to get one before we moved here, but I didn't."

"Oh, too bad. I'm getting one for my birthday this weekend. How come you didn't get yours?"

"It just didn't happen." The explanation was too complicated and too revealing, and her disappointment too razor-edged to handle.

Still Joy looked at Leeann sympathetically and said, "I'd die if I didn't get a horse now."

"Horses' portraits—not a bad idea. Let's go with it, you guys." The boy who had given his approval was tall and homely with a long jaw and narrow, intelligent eyes. Zach. He was Zach, Leeann reminded herself.

"So what are we going to do, everybody just bring in a report about their horse?" Alan asked. He was sitting on Joy's desk, a compact, handsome boy with strong cheekbones and fine blond hair that flopped into his eyes. He looked at Joy for an answer and she reached up and brushed back the escaped lock of his hair.

Kristen's intense blue eyes took in the intimate gesture, but Leeann couldn't read her expression. Kristen was pretty too, except she wore braces and her black hair was cropped short as a boy's. The two girls made Leeann feel plain. But they seemed friendly enough. Casually she offered, "I could bring in my camera, and we could get a photograph of each horse to go with its story."

"Another neat idea," Joy said. "Hey, Leeann, I'm glad you joined us."

Leeann smiled. Maybe it would be good here, after all. Maybe she'd make friends easily, and surely Amos would relent soon and let her near his horses.

CHAPTER 3 -------------

Leeann was the only one left on the school bus by the time it got to the ranch. The bulldog-faced lady driver gave her a friendly smile and said, "End of my run. See you tomorrow?"

"I expect so," Leeann said. "Thanks." And she swung off.

She stood a minute to study her new home. The wooden sign strung across two tall fence posts at the entrance said, "Lost River Ranch." Hanna hadn't mentioned a river here, lost or not. Leeann wondered if there was a dry bed where a stream had been. She couldn't go near the horses, but exploring to find the riverbed might be interesting.

She walked up the gravel drive toward the main house. The ranch was small, Hanna had said, no more than a couple of dozen guests at a time and usually less. It was closed from May to October because then it was too hot in this part of Arizona for people to ride or for the horses to be ridden. The Holdens made some money from breeding their horses, so somewhere beyond the outbuildings there had to be colts and yearlings too young to be ridden. Their sire was Darth Vader, the horse Amos had warned Leeann not to go near. Should she do her report on him? But who would give her information? Not Amos, unless she could somehow win over that angry old man.

She trudged past the oval of lawn in front of the porch, which was full of comfortable wooden chairs and stretched the whole length of the house. Past the facade, the building sprouted additions, some made of mismatched boards and crooked windows. The cabin that was now home was as small as a one-car detached garage in Charlotte. She didn't care, Leeann told herself. And she didn't even mind having to share a bed with her mother.

But she wished Big John had never promised her a horse. The belief that she was getting one had left a craving in her. Not that Rose could afford a horse even if one magically appeared. Horses cost a lot to maintain, and Rose barely had enough money to cover necessities like car insurance. But practical as Leeann considered herself, she couldn't shed her longing.

The cottage was empty. A note on the table said, "I'll be in the ranch house. Cookies in the cookie jar. Milk in the refrigerator. Love you, Rose."

Leeann ate a cookie and drank a glass of milk. She was never very hungry. If she ate more she might not be so bony, people said, but she had tried and hadn't gained any weight. Rose claimed Leeann had an interesting face. "You'll be a beauty when you're grown," Rose promised. Leeann doubted it. She hoped people would like her because she was diligent and helpful, a useful person. If only Amos would let her prove how useful she could be! It was unfair that he wouldn't allow her to go near the horses. He was a mean man.

She got into old jeans and a faded "Save the Rainforest" T-shirt and started out to find the river. It wouldn't do to bother Rose while she was busy cooking.

The sky in every direction except back toward town was scalloped with hills. Some were oddly shaped with wind-worn rocks that projected from them like fingers or fists against the blueness. No clouds. It was February, yet there were no clouds and it was warm as summer. If they were here next summer, they'd have to get used to the heat. But where would Rose work when the place shut down in May? Life was too full of questions. Leeann wanted something sure, something solid like the big warm body of a horse to hold onto.

In the distance, a string of horses led by Amos crossed the field toward the ranch house. Leeann recognized Amos by his gray ponytail. She waved, ready to tell him she was only going exploring, but he was too far away to call to, and he didn't give any sign of seeing her. The horses Amos was leading were a shabby bunch, too fat, too swaybacked, too angular, too something. None of them was as handsome as the black stud.

Leeann stopped to watch three pretty yearlings playing in a small corral. They were bays, with glossy brown coats and black tails and manes. One bumped another who was watching Leeann and they chased each other around the corral until the bumped horse reared up. The third horse lay down on its back and rolled from side to side in the soft dirt. Leeann pulled up grass from her side of the fence and offered it between the wires. The animals watched her, but they wouldn't come to her even though she spoke to them softly and at length.

Still in search of the riverbed, she hiked along the wire fencing until it turned a corner on a wooden post. Now she was picking her way through prickly pear cactus and low scrubby bushes that looked too dry and thorny to be edible even by a horse. The fence went over a rise and there below her was the riverbed, dry as a dusty road.

A horse stood in it.

This animal was brown with a black tail and mane like the yearlings, but it was older. Sleek and full-chested with long slender legs, it had no obvious defects like the horses Amos had been leading. It was as handsome as the black stud, but not aggressive. This horse looked mischievous.

"Hi, horse, what you doing there all by yourself?" Leeann said. The animal was watching her with ears cocked forward. She moved steadily toward it. It watched her with interest and didn't back away.

"You looking for company?" Leeann asked. "Or are you expecting me to have a treat for you?" She stopped within an arm's length of the horse. It blew out some air and bobbed its head toward her hands. She reached out and touched its forelock. It stepped closer to her. She stroked its forehead and the long slide of its neck. Its soft muzzle bumped her shoulder.

"Hey, you're a friendly one," Leeann said. "You wouldn't be looking for a playmate, would you?" For a long time she petted the animal, who nudged her occasionally in return. It was a male, she observed. She took a few steps back up the rise from the dry riverbed. "I'd better head on home," she said over her shoulder. "Want to come along?"

The bright-eyed animal acted as if he understood her; at least he followed her up the rise. She offered him some grass that he could have perfectly well reached himself. He took the clump politely, and with comical sidewise motions of his lower jaw, ate her offering. "Coming?" she asked. Amazingly, the horse did come. He ambled along with her as if they were companions out for a walk.

Leeann was delighted. "Aren't you the one," she said. "You're some cutie pie, you are. I wish you were mine. I wouldn't even have to ride you to enjoy you." It occurred to her that this animal was docile enough to ride bareback. But she had nothing to steer him with, not even a rope. And what if Amos caught her? Still, when she saw a table-sized rock, she was tempted. She climbed on it and called the horse to her. He came, but on the wrong side.

"This way," Leeann told him. "Come around this side." The horse frisked around the rock, tail swishing, as if he were playing a game. As soon as he happened to come up alongside where Leeann wanted him, she grabbed his mane with one hand and heaved herself belly down across his back. From that position it was easy to swing one leg to the other side and sit up, still holding onto the mane. The horse danced sideways.

"It's all right," Leeann said soothingly. "I'm not that heavy, am I? Want to carry me back to the ranch? Come on. We'll surprise Amos. I bet he'll be glad I'm bringing you home!" Gently she nudged the well-fleshed ribs with her sneakered heels. That started the animal trotting and she almost lost her balance. She had never ridden bareback before, and she was so tickled to find out she could do it that she laughed out loud.

"Hey, horse, slow down and walk, will you?" she told him. "Walk! Please! It's too bouncy when you trot." She sat back and pushed her legs forward. Obediently he slowed to a walk.

She was riding him alongside the fence when she saw Amos again. Now he was leading a line of trail riders up along a ridge to her right. He was looking at her over his shoulder. She pointed to the horse and yelled, "I found him." She could see Amos's shaggy gray eyebrows but not the expression on his face. Maybe he hadn't heard her. Maybe he didn't understand. Her heart revved up alarmingly as she realized that he just might not want to yell at her in front of the guests.

She kept walking her mount toward the ranch. Next time she looked back, Amos and his riders had disappeared behind some rocks. Leeann kept steering the obliging horse with her legs as well as she could toward the main corral.

She slid off when she got to it, figured out how to unlatch the gate, and led the horse into the corral with her hand against his neck. "You're some horse," she said. "You really are. Thanks for the ride."

He nudged her twice in the chest with his head as if to return the compliment, then ambled to the water barrel and began to slurp up water noisily. He'd been thirsty, Leeann realized. That may have been why he'd been willing to return. Well, Amos had to be pleased she'd brought him back. She hoped he'd be pleased enough to forgive her.

Leeann closed the gate behind her and went to find her mother in the kitchen of the big building.

"You don't want to get too fancy," Hanna was saying to Rose as they stood over a slab of beef that Rose was cutting into cubes. "Using a lot of wine and herbs in things won't get you half the compliments that plain grilled steak and maybe some corn bread and fresh string beans will."

"Hi," Leeann said. "This kitchen smells wonderful."

"That's the pies in the oven," Hanna said. "Your ma's doing all the work. I'm just standing here directing her."

"It's not true," Rose said. "Hanna can do more with one hand than I can do with two any day."

"That's what my third husband used to say. He'd sit back and let me do all the work and pay me off in compliments. Took me a while to realize I was being had." Hanna laughed. She'd been married four times, and the longest marriage hadn't lasted a year. She'd never had any children.

Rose said, "You always were a working fool, Hanna."

Hanna was the practical one, Rose had told Leeann. It was Hanna who had talked Rose into staying in college when Rose, the dreamer, had nearly flunked out because she had fallen in love with a boy who aced tests without studying and who dropped her anyway. Hanna had never gone to college herself. "No brains," she'd told Leeann once. But it wasn't so. Hanna was smart enough. She just wasn't interested in any learning she couldn't immediately apply.

They looked as if they were having fun together, Leeann thought. She was glad for her mother. Rose needed some fun in her life.

"School go okay?" Rose asked cautiously.

"Pretty good," Leeann said, although she wasn't

26

that sure about Ms. Morabita. "I'm doing a project on horses with four other kids."

"Wonderful," Rose said. She sounded as if she'd been fearful it was going to be hard for Leeann. "Nice kids?"

"So far they seem nice. I need some information on the horses on this ranch, though. Do you know much about them, Hanna?"

"Me? No. Amos is the one to ask. He knows them like they're his family."

"Amos doesn't like me."

"He doesn't like anybody much. Don't worry. He's not as bad as he looks. It's his arthritis makes him cranky . . . he still mad at you about that business with the stud?"

"Yes, and today he saw me riding a horse I found roaming around in the old riverbed. I brought it back to the corral, but he didn't thank me."

Hanna laughed. "If you found a horse roaming, it must be Sassy. That animal gives Amos fits. Never stays where he puts him."

"This horse came right to me and let me ride him."

"That's Sassy. Short for Sassafras. He's friendly enough, but always leaping fences and going off somewhere so Amos or somebody has to chase after him."

"Really? Well, then why isn't he pleased I brought him back?"

"Tell you what," Hanna said. "You want to make

friends with Amos, you can bring the dessert out to the shed where the cowboys eat. Serve him an extra big piece of apple pie and he'll melt like butter."

"First eat your own dinner," Rose said.

"No rush," Hanna advised. "Those fellows won't be eating for another hour or so. They have to take care of the horses after the last trail ride. Usually we feed the guests first and the cowboys get theirs last."

Dinner was delicious. Tomato stew, scalloped potatoes, and roast chicken with a spinach salad. The meat Rose had been cutting up was meant for the next night's meal. She set it to marinate in a gigantic roasting pan. After eating, Leeann helped with the clean up. Hanna was telling Rose that the Holdens were getting too old to do much besides sit behind the desk, greet guests, and see they paid their bills when they left.

"Don Holden and Amos are both pushing seventy. Maybe Holden's a few years older," Hanna said.

"Are the Holdens going to continue running this ranch?" Rose asked apprehensively.

"Well," Hanna said cheerfully, "she wants him to sell out and retire, but he keeps holding out for another year. I think he'd like to die in the saddle, so to speak. His daddy ran this place before him, and he loves it here. No sense worrying about our jobs till we have to, Rose. Things always work out somehow," Hanna said.

The shed where the cowboys ate had screened windows and a low-pitched roof. Nothing was in it but a long picnic table with benches. Leeann cut Amos an extra large hunk of pie. Robuck, the skinny young cowboy, frowned at that but he didn't say anything. Hank, the middle-aged man with droopy eyelids and a thick mustache, didn't seem to notice her at all.

"I found that horse you saw me riding in the old riverbed," Leeann said to Amos. "He seemed friendly and I figured he was lost. That's why I rode him back."

"Dangerous to pick up with an animal you don't know. You could get kicked or bit or knocked senseless falling off," Amos answered.

"But he was lost, wasn't he?"

"Always is. Can't keep that Sassy inside anything. That's why we still got him. Comes back like a bad penny every time he gets sold."

"He has to be sold? Couldn't he be used for riding? He likes people."

"He likes his own way. Can't trust him to stay in line on a trail."

"Was Sassy born here?" Leeann asked. She was thinking she was getting her research done even if Amos hadn't warmed up to her yet.

"Son of Darth Vader and a mare we had to shoot. Broke her leg before she'd weaned her colt. We had to mother Sassafras too much. That's why he turned out wrong. He don't know he's a horse."

"But if he can jump? Isn't that good for something?"

"Yeah, for making trouble."

"He butted Amos into the water barrel the other day," the skinny kid said. He snickered.

Amos glared at him. "Just keep away from that horse," he said to Leeann.

She asked him if he wanted another slice of pie. "Don't mind if I do," he said mildly. There was one piece left. It wasn't fair not to divide it, but she needed Amos to melt like butter—especially since she had no intention of keeping away from Sassy.

CHAPTER 4 ----------

On Tuesday, Ms. Morabita started off English class with more familiar activities than projects. First came oral book reports and then a lesson on clauses, followed up with worksheets to do for homework. Leeann was reassured. This was the kind of work that came easily to her. It was only in the second hour of their time with her that Ms. Morabita set the class loose on their projects.

Instantly, chairs scraped the floor and the noise level shot up. Leeann was glad she already had a group to join, especially when Joy greeted her by name and patted the desk next to hers in welcome.

"Guess what?" Joy said as Leeann folded her long legs under the desk top. "I went horse shopping last night with my dad and Alan." Leeann's surprise must have been obvious, because Joy explained, "Alan knows a lot about horses. You know, from his sisters. They each have one."

"I'm their stable boy," Alan said. His smile showed even white teeth above the cleft in his chin, and his pearl-buttoned western shirt looked freshly ironed.

31

"You like horses that much?" Leeann asked him.

"Me? No, I'm no horse junkie," Alan said. "My sisters pay me to take care of their animals while they're away at college, and I can ride any time I feel like."

"Lucky you, Alan," Zach said. He was sitting on his desk, hanging over the others like a buzzard or a skinny question mark. "I get up at five and do chores until the school bus comes, and Dad still gives me the same allowance I got in kindergarten."

"Stop your whining," Alan said. "You've saved every nickel of that allowance. You must be rich by now."

"Well, I could *get* rich, maybe, if I win the calf-roping contest at the rodeo next spring," Zach said.

"If you don't break an arm again like you did last year," Kristen put in. Her braces flashed when she smiled, but so did a pair of dimples.

"Last year I was puny. This year I've been working out." Zach pumped up a skinny arm to show a tennis ball–sized muscle. Joy snickered. Zach smiled as if she'd complimented him.

"Zach's crazy," Alan explained to Leeann. "We only put up with him because we know he can't help it."

Zach socked Alan in the arm and said, "Anyhow, I already got my report done. I wrote about our Percherons and how they pulled the dump truck out of the wash."

"I remember that," Kristen said. "It was in the newspaper last winter."

"Yeah, that's where I got my material," Zach admitted. "That reporter got more out of my dad than he tells me in a year. Everything about our horses was in that article."

"Cheater," Alan said. "You're supposed to do research. At least three sources, Morabita said."

"I'll look at the encyclopedia if I have the time," Zach said.

"Most of my stuff'll come out of my journal," Kristen said. "I've written about two hundred pages on my horse, Moley. I've been writing about him ever since I got him, but he was already nineteen then, and I wish I knew what happened to him before."

"You're going to hand in a *two hundred* page journal?" Joy asked.

"No, I'll just copy out the best stuff."

"What are you going to do, Leeann?" Joy asked.

Leeann sighed. "I guess I can write about a horse named Sassafras on the ranch where my mother and I are living. He's a kind of escape artist."

"You're living on a ranch? Which one?" Zach asked.

Leeann told him, and he said, "Oh, yeah. They hire us to do moonlight wagon rides with the Percherons. How come you're there?"

"My mother's friend is the cook. She broke her wrist, so Rose's helping her."

"Your mother's a cook?" Joy asked at the same time as Zach asked, "You call your mother by her first name?"

Leeann answered Zach first. "I always have. She thought it was funny when I started because I was little, and it kind of became a habit." She turned to Joy and said, "Rose isn't a regular cook. She's an interior decorator, sort of. I mean, that's what she studied in college, but . . ."

Leeann shrugged, reluctant to admit that her mother hadn't been able to make a living at interior decorating. "My mother can do lots of stuff. She even had her own upholstery business and she did wallpapering," she finished.

"I could do that," Kristen said. "I helped my mother wallpaper my grandmother's house."

"Kristen's mother runs the campaign against drunk drivers," Zach supplied.

"Mostly she does church work," Kristen said. "*Lots* of church work." Kristen's small earnest face was unreadable, but her emphasis on "lots" sounded negative.

"Your church used to send us casseroles and cakes when my mom first took sick, but they gave up on us. Figures," Zach said. "My dad never did think much of churches. I bet I haven't been in one since I was six."

"Your mom's been sick as long as I've known you," Joy said.

"Yeah," Zach said.

Leeann wondered what was wrong with Zach's mother, but she was shy about asking. Her father had been ill a long time, too. He had begun dying when she was three. Instead of dance class and music lessons, her childhood had been spent in hospital visits and the waiting rooms of doctors' offices. Her father had died when she was eight.

Ms. Morabita appeared. "How are you guys doing?" she asked.

Zach whipped out a spiral notebook scrawled full of notes. "I'm gonna do our Percherons," he said.

"Nice start, Zach," she said. "And how about the rest of you?"

"My horse doesn't even *come* until my birthday Saturday, Ms. Morabita," Joy said.

"You could research different kinds of horses meanwhile," Ms. Morabita suggested. Before she could quiz the rest of them, her attention was diverted to a group who were shooting paper airplanes at each other, and off she went.

"Good job, Zach, you got us off the hook," Alan said.

"Ah, Morabita's okay. It's just that this is her first job, so she's jumpy."

"You know what would be fun," Joy said eagerly. "How about if you all ride your horses over to my house on Saturday so we can fool around in the ring with them?"

"Your father built you a ring already?" Zach asked.

"Don't you know Joy's daddy will do anything for his little princess," Alan said. "He's going to buy her a pricey palomino, too."

"No, he said it was way too expensive," Joy said wistfully.

"You wanna bet it'll be there when you wake up on your birthday?"

Joy cupped her freckled face in her hands. "Oh, I wish," she said with a blissful smile.

Before school ended, Joy drew Leeann a map of how to get to her house. "Try and be there at one," she said when she handed Leeann the instructions.

"But I don't know if I can borrow Sassy. He's not mine, Joy."

"Don't be silly," Joy said. "Your mother works there, doesn't she?" At Leeann's nod, Joy continued blithely, "They'll let you borrow a horse. You know, if you go around the butte, the way I showed you on the map, it's only a couple of miles between your place and mine. We'll be able to ride together whenever we want."

Leeann nodded again. There was no point arguing with Joy. When she didn't show up, she could explain on Monday that Amos wouldn't let her take Sassy. Not that she didn't want to go. She did. She liked Joy. In fact, she liked the whole horse project group. Zach was comfortable to talk to. Kristen seemed overly serious but nice.

As for Alan, he was the kind of cool, good-looking boy who usually made Leeann nervous, but since he was Joy's boyfriend, he didn't bother her. If only she had the use of a horse, she'd be part of a group.

Leeann was daydreaming about the horse Big John would send her as an apology for deserting her and her mother when the school bus lurched to a stop and the driver started yelling out the window. "Get out of the way, you four-footed fool. Can't you see this bus is bigger than you?"

Past the driver's shoulder, Leeann could see Sassy standing broadside to the bus in the road ahead of them. She guessed it was Sassy because of the inquisitive expression on the animal's face as he chewed a clump of long grass and regarded the bus. The grass extended from either side of his mouth like green whiskers. The bus driver tooted her horn. Sassy's lip wrinkled back to show his teeth in a goofy-looking smile as he worked on the scraggly grass. But he didn't budge from the middle of the road.

"I'll get him out of the way," Leeann offered when the bus driver began spluttering angrily at the animal.

"Go to it," the driver said.

She released the door and Leeann swung off the steps, calling, "Here Sassy, here boy. You don't want to get hit, do you?"

Sassy peered over his shoulder at Leeann, then stepped toward her, bobbing his head in a friendly way. Leeann rubbed his mushroom-soft nose while the driver angled the bus around his hindquarters, which still protruded into the road.

"Do you do this often?" Leeann asked him. "Block traffic, I mean? I know it must be fun to stop such a big machine, but you could get hurt. I mean really, you could."

Sassy snuffled, brushing Leeann's cheek with the remaining grass ends. It wasn't far to the ranch. "Go on," Leeann told the driver. "I'll walk Sassy home."

"Better that than me having to give that horse a ride," the driver joked and took off.

It was the second time Leeann was returning Sassy to the corral for Amos and she hadn't been there a full week. He had to appreciate her usefulness. But when Amos saw her coming toward him with her arm slung over Sassy's neck, he glowered and asked, "What you doing with that horse now?"

"I'm not doing anything. My school bus almost hit him. He was in the road."

Amos kicked the gate open. "We don't sell him soon, he's gonna break a leg and make himself worthless." Amos slapped Sassy's flank and slammed the gate shut after the horse trotted into the corral. Not that it mattered. Sassy had already proven he could jump out when he felt like it.

"I was wondering," Leeann began. "Would it be all right if I—"

Amos was halfway to the door marked "office" in the ranch house. "I'm too busy to talk to you now, girl," he said.

So much for gratitude, Leeann thought. If she wanted a horse to ride to Joy's on Saturday, she'd have to steal one.

Sassy had stayed put on the other side of the gate. "Want to get stolen and go for a ride with me?" Leeann asked him.

The bright eyes watching her were so full of mischief that the answer was obvious.

"The thing is, I'd have to steal a saddle and bridle as well, and that would be sort of hard and more like really *stealing*. Well, let me think about it. Okay?" Leeann said to Sassy.

She laughed when the long brown head shook up and down. Even if Sassy was just ridding himself of a fly, the timing was incredible.

CHAPTER 5 ----------------

The kitchen of the big ranch house was long and furnished with rough wooden shelves and scarred wooden counters. A chorus line of pots and pans hung from the ceiling. The tangy scent of chicken grilled over mesquite sweetened the air, which was steamy from the dinner Rose and Hanna had cooked for the guests. Leeann felt good to be part of the action as she loaded the commercial-sized dishwasher. A commotion outside made her glance out the open kitchen door.

The moon lit the shadowy corral area. Beside it, like an apparition from pioneer days, was a wagon drawn by two enormous pale horses with white manes, but the horses were too solid to be ghosts. Intrigued, Leeann set the last dirty dish in place and slipped out to investigate.

She was hailed by a vaguely familiar voice. "Leeann, I got something for you."

"Zach?" He stepped off the ramada at the front of the ranch house into the shaft of moonight, and she realized the big horses were his father's

Percherons. "What are you doing here?" she asked him.

"Pop's got business with Mr. Holden." Zach nodded toward the horses. "We came by wagon to give Peter and Paul practice hauling people instead of machines." Zach went over to the wagon and reached under some bags. "Here," he said, holding out to her with both hands a lightweight saddle with a bridle wrapped around it. "You said you might could get hold of a horse but not a saddle. This is my mom's, so it's just a loaner. Okay?"

Now Leeann remembered confiding to him on the ball field at school while they were waiting their turn at bat why she probably wouldn't be able to get to Joy's on Saturday. She'd guessed that Zach would understand, because it seemed that he, like her, had fewer things that cost money than the others in their group.

"Zach, that's so nice of you," Leeann said now. "But I don't think I should. I mean, your mother's saddle . . ."

"She'll never use it again," he said curtly. "I would've asked her and she would've said sure, but I didn't want her mentioning it to Pop. He's funny about stuff that belongs to her."

"What's wrong with your mother?"

"Multiple sclerosis. She's been in a wheelchair four years now."

"I'm sorry."

He shrugged. "She says it's not so bad. She likes

looking at birds, so I keep the feeder filled for her."

"But who takes care of her?"

"Pop and me mostly. We feed her. The county sends a lady to bathe her and do stuff like that."

"That's got to be hard on you." Leeann remembered her mother's exhaustion in the last year of her father's life, when he had been bedridden.

"Nah. I'm used to it. And Mom's not a complainer. She says she's blessed to be able to watch me growing up. And up and up and up." He grinned. "My mom's a real sweetheart."

"But if your father finds out about the saddle . . ." Leeann pushed it back toward him. She didn't want Zach getting in trouble because of her.

"Not to worry. If he found out, Pop'd grumble at me, that's all. Basically we get along fine."

Men's voices resounded from the darkness of the ramada.

"So it's a deal, then?" The stranger's voice was deep as a well.

Mr. Holden's sounded high by comparison as he answered, "So long as you take care of the campfire, it's a deal, Sam. Moonlight rides on the desert are a real drawing card. The ladies think it's romantic to lie down in a bunch of straw and be bumped around in the night." Mr. Holden chuckled.

Zach's father stepped into the light. He was built like his horses. Tall, skinny Zach looked fragile by comparison. Zach stood so that the saddle was hidden behind him. He nudged an elbow at Leeann, and she took the saddle and ducked behind the building before his father could see what she was carrying. She felt guilty about borrowing the saddle and wondered how much risk Zach really was taking for her. Well, she'd be sure to return his mother's tack promptly after Saturday.

Now the big question was if she could catch Sassy when she needed him. Tonight he had stayed quietly in the corral with the other horses. Unpredictable was the word for Sassy.

In their cabin that night, Leeann asked her mother, "If a boy takes a risk for you, does that mean he likes you?"

"I expect it does." Rose's warm amber eyes rested on her daughter.

"Likes you especially? I mean more than any other girl?"

"I don't know, Leeann. What risk did this boy take?"

"Oh, never mind," Leeann said. Considering that she was just a tall, thin girl with ordinary features, it wasn't likely that Zach was attracted to her. Probably he was just goodhearted. Probably that was it.

"Have you found yourself a boyfriend already?" Rose persisted, smiling.

Leeann had always confided her crushes to her mother. They'd started as far back as second grade when she'd dropped anonymous gifts on a boy's desk at school and sent him an unsigned valentine card. It had seemed safer to like someone without letting him know it to save being hurt if he didn't seem to like her back.

"I doubt it," Leeann answered Rose now. "Sassy's the only one I'm gone on so far."

Rose laughed. "Good," she said. "A horse shouldn't give me nearly as much to worry about as a boy."

Leeann wasn't sure Rose was right, especially if she got into trouble stealing Sassy, which was what she meant to do rather than risk having Amos refuse to let her take him. It shouldn't be that hard to steal him. Amos was so used to Sassy disappearing that he wouldn't even realize the animal was gone. And if he happened to see Leeann returning to the ranch with Sassy, she could say she'd just found him wandering and brought him back again. Leaving was the only tricky part. Sassy would have to cooperate by going out of sight of the main buildings before Leeann tried to catch and saddle him.

One good thing about Zach, Leeann thought as she showered in the rusty metal stall in the bathroom, was that he was as tall as she. Even though he was kind of homely, with his long jaw and nose, she liked him a lot. Not as much as she

44

liked Sassy, but enough so that her nerve endings tingled when she was near him.

Saturday morning Hanna told Leeann that on Amos's day off, he usually took a long ride out to some canyon or other—unless he had to go to Tucson for arthritis treatments. "Sometimes the poor man can barely haul himself onto a horse's back. He won't give in to it, though. Says he can't afford not to work. No insurance, no benefits. Nobody to take care of him, and nothing saved up for his old age."

Hanna shook her head in sympathy. But Hanna probably wasn't any better off, Leeann thought. And neither was Rose. Of course, the women were still relatively young and strong, so they didn't have to worry yet. And Rose had her. Leeann intended to take care of her mother as soon as she got old enough to earn a living.

Even if Amos had a good excuse for his grouchiness, Leeann was wary of him and kept an eye peeled for both him and Sassy. She'd hidden Zach's saddle across the road from the ranch behind a mass of prickly pear cactus. It was tangled up with mistletoe that was growing on a dead tree and was right on the route she'd be traveling, according to Joy's map. Leeann had told her mother she was going to Joy's house for a few hours. Since Rose was concentrating—under Hanna's direction—on the proper technique for mixing biscuits, she forgot to ask how Leeann proposed to get there.

Locating Sassy was the next step. Leeann sniffed in disgust when she saw how easy and how hard it was going to be. There Sassy was in plain sight in the main corral, the only horse left. He was pulling at hay from the huge wire feeding silo, which was protected from rain and sun by a wooden canopy.

"Sassy," Leeann called from the corral gate. The horse ignored her. "Did you leap this fence to get back in just because you're not supposed to be here?" Leeann asked. The horse continued munching. Leeann whistled. Sassy looked up, then went back to eating.

Stealing him from the corral would be impossible in full view of the ramada, which was at its busiest this morning. Cars were parked all over the place, with guests either packing up to leave or unloading to check in, and Robuck was there, busy doing extra duty as bellhop.

"Sassy," Leeann called. "Here, Sassy." She whistled louder. The horse looked over his shoulder inquiringly, then went back to pulling at the hay. What if he felt like spending the whole day munching away?

Leeann waited for him to get tired of eating. It was hot in the sun and she didn't have a hat. Sassy was probably cool, comfortable and content under the canopy. Leeann sighed and walked back to the cabin for the straw hat Rose used outdoors to shade her sensitive skin. When Leeann returned to the corral, it was empty.

Now where had that horse gone? It was time to leave if she was to get to Joy's on time. Leeann started her search by following the fence uphill to the fields where the horses were spread out, grazing on whatever patches of green they could find. Plenty of brown horses with black manes and tails were about, but none with a mischievous sparkle in its eyes.

Amos had forbidden her to go through the gate into the fields. Instead Leeann climbed over the hill and down to the dry riverbed where she'd found Sassy the first time. A small black bird with a pointy crest flew from the fence to a nearby tree. The bird was the only sign of life in the riverbed.

Where was Sassy? Even with the hat to protect her, the sun pressed insistently against Leeann's back and shoulders. If she were a horse, she'd be looking for shade, someplace high and breezy. She considered the track out toward the buttes where she'd seen Amos leading trail rides. It was as good a place as any to search, and it led through cactuses and scrawny trees with little leaves that didn't provide much protection from the sun but were better than nothing. The first hill turned out to be higher than she'd expected, and Leeann was panting by the time she got to the top. She wasn't sweating, though; the air was too dry for perspiration to gather.

From the top of the hill, she could see back to the ranch and past it to creased and crumpled mountains against the horizon. To her right she saw a picnic table under a thatched roof, and to the left what looked like a canyon leading off from the river bottom below her. If she'd followed the riverbed it would have taken longer, but she wouldn't have had to climb, she thought. Then she spotted Sassy. The horse was pawing at something in the riverbed on the far side of its curve around the hill. Leeann headed downhill straight toward him, knocking bits of gravel that clinked as they rolled ahead of her. Sassy looked over his shoulder, ears quirking forward, more interested than alarmed at Leeann's approach.

"Hi, there," Leeann said. "Want to go visiting with me?"

Sassy wore a bell on a leather thong around his neck this morning, probably to make him easier to find when Amos wanted him. "Come on," Leeann said, tugging at the bell. "It's an adventure. You'll like it."

Sassy whoofed as if to scoff, but he began ambling along easily enough when Leeann started walking. She led him via the riverbed back toward the ranch. "Let's hope we don't meet Amos. If we do, I'll say I found you and am bringing you back like before. If we don't find him, though, I'm going to walk you straight across the road to where I've got the tack hidden and hope nobody yells 'stop thief.'"

Sassy stopped to nibble at a clump of grass. Leeann waited patiently. "I know it's your day off," she said, "but you don't work that hard. Hanna says half the time Amos can't find you and has to use some other horse. A little ride over to Joy's house shouldn't be any problem for you, right?"

They were passing the barn. No one seemed to notice her walking down the driveway, no one who was employed on the ranch, anyway. Leeann was sensitive to the noisy *clip clop, clip clop* of Sassy's hooves as they crossed the asphalt road, but not a car or truck was in sight. On they went, into the cactus-studded wasteland toward the butte Joy had said to use as a landmark. When they reached the sprawling prickly pear behind which Leeann had hidden Zach's saddle and bridle, Leeann relaxed.

"You're sure easy to steal," she told Sassy, who nudged her companionably as if he were enjoying their escapade. Leeann took off the bell and exchanged it for the bridle. On the route home, she'd reverse the procedure and stow the saddle there again. Sassy took the bit into his mouth without protest, and Leeann slid the headstall over his ears. The saddle was light enough to toss onto his back easily. Leeann cinched the girth and stepped into the dangling stirrup. There, she was mounted. Sassy started walking before Leeann had adjusted her stirrups.

"Ho," Leeann said and pulled back on the reins. Sassy stopped obediently. "Good boy," Leeann told him. "For a horse with such a mind of your own, you're pretty easy to ride."

She took the map out of her back pocket. It seemed simple enough to circle the butte and then head toward the road on the other side of it and walk along that to Joy's house. Joy said her house had a bright red, yellow, and blue playhouse and slide in the yard that her brother loved. Leeann wondered how old Joy's brother was. A toddler probably. She wished she had a little brother, but as things stood, Rose had enough to manage with just one child.

To keep Sassy entertained, Leeann whistled as they went. Sassy's ears turned back to hear her. Leeann was getting excited now that it seemed she was actually going to pull off this caper. It would be interesting to see Joy's home and meet Kristen's beloved Moley, and it would be fun to spend an afternoon with both horses and friends. Besides, Zach would be there.

As for getting Sassy back without being caught, no point worrying about that until she had to, Leeann decided.

CHAPTER 6 ----------------

Joy's handsome, white, one-story house sparkled as if it were newly painted. It was surrounded by a latticework fence of white concrete block. The playhouse and slide in red, yellow, and blue plastic stuck out incongruously just as Joy had described them.

Leeann laid the right rein lightly over Sassy's neck. Obediently, the horse turned into the crescent-shaped driveway and ambled around the house to the back where flowering plants in clay pots outlined a patio set in a lawn. It was the first lawn Leeann had seen in this desert community, aside from the small oval in front of the ramada at the ranch.

One of Zach's Percherons was already tied to the skinny metal railing around the corral to the right of the lawn. Inside the ring, a wheat-colored palomino frisked about, swishing its blond tail. So Alan had been right about Joy's father getting her the horse she wanted, Leeann thought. The palomino was beautiful. Its compact body flowed as smoothly as rippling water as it sidestepped daintily on slender legs.

"Some horse, huh?" Zach asked. He emerged from Joy's house carrying a thermos and paper cups. Joy followed him with a tray of cookies.

"Gorgeous!" Leeann said with genuine admiration.

"I mean Paul, my horse," Zach teased. "You ever see shoulders like his? He could pull apart a mountain with those muscles."

Leeann laughed and admitted, "Paul's beautiful, too. In his own way." She swung off Sassy and tied him to the top rail of the corral. "You are, too, fella," she murmured in his ear in case the amiable animal was feeling slighted. "Can I help with anything?" she asked Joy.

"No, thanks, we're done," Joy said. She and Zach set the refreshments on a picnic table outside the ring. "Come let me introduce you to Rabbit. Isn't that an awful name for a horse?"

The palomino backed away from them in wide-eyed alarm when they joined him in the ring. "He's not used to me yet," Joy said.

"He's really graceful," Leeann said. "You could rename him Dancer."

"Dancer. I like that," Joy said.

"Jeremiah'd be better," Zach said straight-faced.

"Zach's big on biblical names," Joy said. "Him and Kristen's grandmother. Which incidentally— Kristen's not coming because her grandmother got mad at her for something again, so Kristen has to copy a page out of the Bible. That's what her grandmother always makes her do. And if Kristen makes the least little mistake, she has to keep copying until she gets it perfect."

"Which explains why the girl's handwriting is so great," Zach said.

"Come on, Zach," Joy protested. "You know Kristen's grandma's mean to her. My dad says that lady's a fanatic. She thinks anybody who disagrees with her is going straight to hell. And she's sure anybody outside of her own church will pollute Kristen."

"Nobody much around here *goes* to her church," Zach said.

"Actually, we're the only friends Kristen has," Joy told Leeann. "And she isn't allowed to see us after school."

"That *is* mean," Leeann said.

"Well, once in a while her mother brings her over to do homework with me. And she's allowed to come to my birthday parties."

"Last year, Kristen's grandma wouldn't let her be an angel in the school play. She said it was blasphemous," Zach said.

"But doesn't Kristen's mother decide anything?" Leeann asked.

"Not in that house. The grandmother runs the show because she's got the money," Zach said. "Disobey her and they go on bread and water."

Joy gave him a shove and said, "Don't listen to

Zach. He exaggerates everything." Thoughtfully, she added, "In my family, Dad earns the money and Mom decides how to spend it."

They all turned at the sound of someone squealing, "Joy-ee, Joy-ee, Joy-ee!" A boy was running toward them as awkwardly as a two-year-old. His hands flapped in the air in front of his chest, but he wasn't a toddler. He was shorter than Joy but looked older somehow because of his large head and high, naked forehead.

"Careful, Joey. Don't run or you'll fall," Joy cautioned.

"I want a cookie, Joy-ee," he said as he came up to them. "Ma said."

"Sure, Joey." Joy slipped out between the railings of the corral. She got the tray of cookies and held it out to him.

His still-raised hands jerked about as he stared big-eyed at the tray. Anxiously he said, "You pick, Joy-ee."

She gave him a plain butter cookie and his face crumpled in dismay. "Not that one, not that one!"

Joy put the cookie back, "Point to the one you want, Joey," she said patiently.

"I want, I want, I want." He hugged himself in his excitement.

She offered him one with a white icing design on it. "This one?"

"Yes, yes, yes." He smiled, open-mouthed. His face relaxed again.

"Now, what do you say?"

"Thank you, Joy-ee."

"Say hi to my friends," Joy said to him. "This is Zach. You know Zach with the big horses?"

"Yes. *Big* horses." Joey flung his arms wide.

"And this is my new friend, Leeann," Joy said.

Leeann had never talked to a disabled child before, never even been close to one. Gravely she said, "I'm pleased to meet you, Joey."

"You know my name," he said with delight.

"Can you say Leeann?" Joy asked.

"Lee-ann," Joey parroted.

"So, do you want to stay and watch us ride?" Joy asked him.

"No." Still smiling, Joey shook his head, but he didn't move away.

"Just be sure you don't come inside the ring. Okay, Joey?" Joy instructed her brother.

"Is Alan coming?" Leeann asked.

"Probably, but he's always late," Joy said. "He hates getting up in the morning, and then he takes forever with his sisters' horses."

"Alan's only a horse person because all the women in his life are," Zach said. He was massaging Sassy's chin to the horse's evident delight. Sassy wrinkled up his nose and showed his teeth as if he were laughing.

"Sassy's a love," Leeann said. "He didn't give me a minute's trouble riding him over here."

When Zach stopped rubbing, Sassy pushed his

shoulder. Joey laughed and said, "Nice horsey. I like him."

A pleasant-faced blond man who was unmistakably Joy's father came up to the ring and leaned on the railing near Joey. "Came out to see what's got your brother so interested," the man said.

Joy introduced him to Leeann. "Fine-looking horse you've got there," Joy's father said politely.

"Oh, Sassy isn't mine. He belongs to the Holdens. They own the ranch where I'm living." Leeann gulped after she'd blurted out that news. Now she was in for it. If Joy's father called the Holdens, he'd know and they'd know she was a horse thief. Suddenly she was struck by the seriousness of what she'd done.

Joy's father, however, had switched his interest from her to Joy, who was attempting to get a bridle on the palomino. The animal kept jerking his head nervously and backing away from her.

"Need help?" her father asked.

"Please, Daddy," Joy said. The palomino's ears were back. "He didn't do this when we bought him."

"No, he didn't. He's probably upset being in a new place. Besides, he doesn't know you yet, honey." Mr. Childs bent and slid between the railings to get into the ring. He put his hands on the palomino's neck and stroked him, talking to the horse in a deep, murmurous voice that seemed to calm him. Then he helped Joy get the bridle over the palomino's head.

Once he had the horse saddled, he gave Joy a boost onto his back.

"Okay up there?" Mr. Childs asked. The palomino kept backing away and sidestepping.

"I think so," Joy said uneasily.

"You look good on him," her father said. "Both of you have the same color hair."

Joy laughed.

"Me, me, me," Joey cried, stretching his splayed-out hands toward his family.

"You better stay outside the ring with us, Joey," Zach said. "Want to say hello to Paul?" He pointed at his horse.

"No." Joey backed up, although he was already a good distance from the massive, white-faced animal whose rear quarters were spotted with black.

"Want to pet my horse, Joey?" Leeann asked him. She touched Sassy, who was standing quietly beside her.

Warily the boy extended his hands to Leeann. She walked over to him and gently drew him close enough so that he could put his hand on Sassy's sleek brown side. Sassy looked back inquiringly. "Doesn't he have beautiful brown eyes, and look how long his eyelashes are," Leeann said. "I think he likes you, Joey."

"Like me?"

Leeann nodded. "I think he does."

Joey put his other hand against the horse voluntarily and then leaned his cheek against Sassy's ribcage. "Tickles," he said.

Zach laughed. Leeann put her cheek against the horse's neck farther up. "It does," she said. "You're right Joey. It tickles."

"Horsey, horsey," Joey yelled, and he jumped up and down.

"That's the first horse I've ever seen Joey take to," Joy's father said. He was still standing beside the palomino, stroking the horse to calm it. "He's always been too scared even to touch one."

"Sassy's very well behaved—at least near people," Leeann said, allowing for Sassy's habit of disappearing from where he was put.

"Think Sassy would give you both a ride around the ring if I put Joey up in the saddle with you?" Joy's father asked eagerly.

"Dad's been trying to get Joey interested in horses for years," Joy explained. "He wants the whole family to go trail riding together."

"Well, we can try," Leeann said. She stepped into the stirrup and pushed herself back until she was seated behind the saddle. Sassy didn't seem to mind, although having a rider in that position had to feel strange to him. Meanwhile, Joy's father came out of the ring and lifted his son up to the level of the horse's back. "Get your leg over on the other side, Joey. No, the other leg, son, the other leg. There you go."

Automatically, Leeann reached around Joey to hold onto the saddle horn. This turned her arms into railings that held Joey in place. Mr. Childs had the reins; he opened the gate and led Sassy inside the ring.

"I ride. I ride," Joey squealed, waving his hands in the air. He was wriggling in his excitement and Leeann had to struggle to keep him in place on the saddle.

"You have to sit still, Joey," she said. "Riders sit still and the horse walks. Can you sit still?"

"Yes, yes, yes," Joey said. He hunched into himself, clasping his hands against his stomach.

Mr. Childs was walking alongside his son on the railing side of the ring. Without being asked, Zach came into the ring and took a position on the opposite side of Sassy in case Joey fell that way.

"How does it feel?" Joy asked Joey.

"High," Joey said. They all laughed.

Once around the ring they went, and then again once more. Joey's body began sagging against Leeann. "How you doing, sport?" his father asked.

"Down," he whined. "Down."

"He's tired," Mr. Childs said. He reached up and lifted Joey off the horse. "I'll take him up to his mother. Can you kids manage alone here?"

"We're fine, Daddy," Joy said. "We'll stay in the ring, and you come back with your camera and take some pictures of us, okay?" Her palomino had finally settled down and was walking in line with

Sassy around the ring. "Hurry up, Zach," Joy said. "I think this horse likes company."

"I don't know if Paul'll fit in that ring," Zach said, but he unhitched the Percheron from the railing and heaved himself up into the saddle.

"Thanks for giving Joey a ride, Leeann," Mr. Childs said. He was holding a weary-looking Joey by the hand. "That was really special. I wonder, could I pay you to bring Sassy over here again to do some more riding with him?"

Leeann gulped. She explained honestly, "I don't think so. I borrowed Sassy just for today, sort of without permission."

She waited for him to scold her as an adult to a child, but he didn't. All he said was, "I'll call Don Holden and speak to him about it. Don't worry. I won't give you away."

Joy's palomino backed around until he was facing Zach's Percheron, who seemed to loom over him. The palomino began tossing his head and fidgeting. Joy squealed. "What do I do now, Daddy?"

"Let them get acquainted," he said.

Unconcerned, Sassy dipped his head through the rails to get at the higher grass outside. Paul began plodding around the ring while Zach worked the reins and talked to him. The palomino sidestepped toward the stolid Percheron, who ignored the smaller animal. Finally, Joy got her horse turned around to follow Paul.

"Mom-my," Joey suddenly began to wail.

"Okay, feller. I know you're tired. Let's go." Mr. Childs picked up his son and carried him to the house.

Leeann touched Sassy lightly with her heel, and they fell into place in the ring behind the palomino.

"I'm going to call him Dancer," Joy said to Leeann when her mount finally settled down and began cooperating with her signals. "You're right; it's a good name for him."

Carefully Zach got to his knees on his broad-backed horse. When he stood up, Joy squealed, "What are you doing, Zach?"

"Taking in the view. Anybody want to try it?" He had both arms out for balance. Now he folded them across his chest and just stood there, rocking slightly with the horse's motion.

"Get down, you fool," Joy said.

Leeann was amused by Zach's circus performance. But that didn't stop her from worrying about what was going to happen when Joy's father called Mr. Holden. If Mr. Childs slipped and gave her away as he talked about his son wanting to ride Sassy, she'd be in big trouble.

What would Mr. Holden and Amos do to her? She imagined Amos's thundercloud face if he found out that she had taken Sassy off the ranch without permission. Amos would never let her near another of his horses.

"I think I should head home," Leeann said. And when Joy protested, Leeann said, "Really, I have to go."

"You haven't even had any punch or cookies."

"Don't worry," Leeann said with a smile. "Zach will eat mine."

Zach groaned. "Just because I stole her potato chips at lunch."

Leeann reached down to open the gate so she and Sassy could leave the ring. Both Zach and Joy seemed disappointed that she was going, but she had lost her appetite for fun. Her urge now was to get Sassy back to Lost River Ranch where he belonged.

"Bye. Have fun. See you in school." Leeann waved and set off.

Two cars and a pickup drove past her as she made toward the shortcut. And there came Alan cantering toward Joy's house on a lathered-up Appaloosa. He swept off his cowboy hat and waved it at Leeann as he swerved into Joy's driveway. She had to eat the dust cloud he'd made all the way to her turnoff into the desert.

The overgrown cactus where she'd stowed the saddle was a welcome sight. She unsaddled Sassy and exchanged the saddle and bridle for the bell Sassy had been wearing that morning to make him easier to locate.

"Well," Leeann told the horse, who clopped along peacefully beside her, "you made some friends today. But Amos is likely to kill me if he catches me bringing you back." She wondered if he'd believe she'd found Sassy wandering. What was Joy's father going to say to Mr. Holden? The more Leeann thought about it, the more appalled she was at the stupid risk she'd taken just for an afternoon's pleasure.

No one was in sight at the ranch. While Sassy took a long drink from the water barrel outside the barn, Leeann borrowed a brush from the tack room and gave him a good grooming. Could she really be so lucky that no one had seen her? Leeann asked herself as she let Sassy into the corral. If she were, she'd never try anything like this again. Never. Whatever craziness had taken hold of her was gone for good.

She found her mother trying out a recipe for banana cake in the ranch house kitchen. Tonight, when they were alone in their cabin, would be the right time to confess that she'd become a horse thief, Leeann decided.

CHAPTER 7 ————————————————

Leeann had dinner in the kitchen with Hanna and Rose that evening, but she ate without any appetite. She was still wondering how she had managed to convince herself that "borrowing" Sassy was a minor misdemeanor equivalent to a white lie.

Amos had told her not to go near the horse, and he was in charge of it. He had every right to be furious with her. How could she have been so willful when she'd always behaved well, as much for her own self-respect as to please her mother? Her brain must have shut down without warning.

As if she could read Leeann's mind, Hanna asked her, "How's it going between Amos and you?"

Leeann bit her lip. "Not good."

"Come on, then. Let's you and me go have our dessert with the cowboys." Over Leeann's protests, Hanna pulled her along to the shed off the kitchen where the staff ate. Rose followed with a large glass dish of peach cobbler.

"We got to get Amos better acquainted with you, Leeann," Hanna explained on the way.

"This isn't the best time," Leeann cautioned.

"Nonsense," Hanna insisted. "Suppertime's always the best time with these guys."

Once she'd steered Leeann into the shed, Hanna gave a hearty greeting to Amos, who didn't even look up. "Have you fellas met Leeann?" she asked stringy Robuck and silent Hank. They both nodded and Robuck said, "Hi," then dropped his eyes shyly.

"So what about the cooking lately? Think Rose here's doing right by you?" Hanna asked with unabated enthusiasm.

"Good chicken," Robuck said.

Hanna was still trying to mine compliments for Rose from the silent men when Mr. Holden stepped into the shed.

"Could I speak to you in private?" he asked Rose.

"Of course." Rose set down the dish of cobbler and turned to follow Mr. Holden out. Over her shoulder she raised a questioning eyebrow at Hanna, who shrugged as if to say she had no idea.

Leeann knew. It was her criminal behavior Mr. Holden wanted to see her mother about. She put her fork down without tasting her dessert and waited. What would they say? What would she say? She gulped and looked at Amos, who had finished his cobbler and was reaching for more. His expression was no more hostile than usual. Maybe it wasn't what she thought. Maybe . . . but there was Rose in the doorway, her face flushed with embarrassment. "Leeann, would you come here, please."

She followed her mother's plump back. When they were alone in the hall of the main building outside the cave-dark library, which was also the television room, Rose stopped and asked in a whisper, "Did you take that horse and ride it somewhere today?"

"Yes," Leeann said.

"Oh, Leeann! If you'd just been patient, Hanna would have done something for you." Rose shook her head and led the way through the library door. Mr. Holden was leaning against the stone fireplace. Two big Hopi Kachina dolls in fierce feathers and paint stood on the mantel on either side of his head. Not a good omen, Leeann thought.

"Now, Leeann," Mr. Holden began in his high drawl, "a member of my staff told me something about you, and first off, I want to know if it's true. Where did you go this afternoon?"

"To Joy's house. She's a friend I made in school."

"And how did you get there?"

"On horseback."

"Amos gave you permission to use one of the horses?"

"No. I—" She was going to say found, but out came the more damning word. "I took Sassy. He likes me. You see, I found him in the wash the day we came here and I brought him back to the corral. Then I found Sassy again when he jumped the fence and wandered off. He always acts like he's glad to see me and he follows me willingly, so I just sort of borrowed him." She took a deep breath and was silent.

"Borrowing a horse without permission is a serious offense, Leeann," Mr. Holden said. "We can't tolerate that kind of behavior. It undermines Amos's authority and it's just plain wrong for you to mess with a horse you don't own." His fine-boned face had set into grim lines.

"I won't ever do anything like that again. I mean, I'm sorry. I don't know what got into me." Leeann's cheeks felt hot; her mother's were flaming.

"See, it's tough on me," Mr. Holden said, "because Amos claims he'll quit if he catches you near his horses again, and he's bullheaded enough to do it. I *need* Amos, Leeann."

"Yes, I'm really sorry."

"So you're to forget there are horses on this ranch until further notice. Understand?"

"Yes." She nodded.

"All right then." Mr. Holden gave Rose an apologetic glance and said, "I'm sorry. I don't like starting off this way with your daughter. I'm sure she's basically as good a girl as you say. But it's going to take some doing to get Amos to trust her after this. And the fact is, a cook's easier to get than a head wrangler as reliable as Amos." Mr. Holden smiled wryly. "Also, he's due some loyalty after thirty years in my employ."

"Of course," Rose said, still red-cheeked with embarrassment.

Leeann wanted to sink into the floor and disappear.

Neither she nor her mother said anything to each other about the situation until they were alone in their cabin. Rose kicked off her shoes and leaned back against the sprung cushions on the love seat facing the kitchen table. Then Leeann asked, "How did Mr. Holden find out?"

"Seems one of the wranglers was driving back to the ranch, and he saw you riding Sassy down some road miles from here."

"It's not that far." Robuck or Hank must have passed her on the short bit of road in front of Joy's house. There had been some traffic on that road, Leeann remembered.

"Well, it's just too bad. I'm sorry, Leeann. I led you to expect you'd get plenty of horseback riding out of my taking this job. And now . . ."

"I know. I ruined it for myself, Mama." Leeann shook her head in dismay.

"Listen," her mother said. "If you're miserable here, and Amos doesn't relent soon, I'll just look for another job somewhere. It's not like being a cook is a career change I'd planned."

"Don't worry about me," Leeann hastened to reassure her. "At least the kids here are friendly."

"It's my fault anyway," Rose said. "If I hadn't been such a fool, we'd still have our lives in Charlotte. I should have known Big John was too good to be true." Rose was wringing her hands.

"I believed in him, too, Mama," Leeann said, and they hugged each other fiercely.

Lying in bed that night, Leeann thought of how it would be for her here without horses. The cabin was too tiny to spend much time in, but she could take walks through the desert. She could read and watch TV in the library in the main house. She could talk to her new friends.

Then it occurred to her that she might not have friends without the use of a horse. Everyone in her project was busy with a horse or horses in one way or another. What did she have in common with them now that she was barred from going near Sassy or any other horse on the ranch? Stupid, she told herself. She'd been so stupid she deserved to suffer for it, and she would. No question about that.

Monday morning Leeann retrieved Zach's saddle and bridle from behind the overgrown prickly pear before the school bus came.

"You going horseback riding or to school?" the bus driver asked her in a friendly way.

"School, unfortunately," Leeann said.

The driver laughed. "I know what you mean," she said. And Leeann let her think she did.

Zach walked down the hall toward her as Leeann came in lugging the saddle with her books piled on top of it. "I hope you can find someplace to stow this, Zach. I just realized it won't fit in my locker too well."

"The secretary will let me stow it in the office," Zach said. "She's soft on me."

"Really? How come?" Leeann teased as if the reason weren't evident.

"'Cause I helped her get her car started once," he answered seriously. He took the saddle from her and Leeann retrieved her books from it.

"Thanks so much for lending it to me. Saturday was fun," she said.

"Yeah, but what'll you do for a saddle next time you go riding?"

"No need to worry about that. I got caught. I'm forbidden to go anywhere near the horses on Lost River Ranch."

"Oh-oh, trouble, huh?"

She nodded. "Did your father notice the saddle was gone?"

"Nah. I was lucky. Usually he notices everything."

"Would he have been mad at you?"

Zach smiled sheepishly. "Yeah. He gets mad easy nowadays. Especially if it's to do with my mom. But mostly we get along. Pop and I are a good team, you know? I haul my end of things and he'll give a grunt and that means, 'Thanks, Zach.' Two grunts and I feel proud of myself for a week."

Leeann was thinking that it was just as well she wouldn't be needing the saddle again. She didn't want Zach getting into trouble for her sake. "Anyway," she said. "I can still do the report on

Sassy. They can't stop me from watching him and writing up how he behaves."

Joy came running down the hall in pursuit of Alan, screeching, "Stop thief!"

Zach reached out and grabbed Alan before he could get by. "What'd he take?" Zach asked as Joy reached them, out of breath with her curly hair in wild disarray. Alan struggled, but he couldn't free himself from Zach's bear hug. Apparently there was strength in those skinny arms

"He's got my diary," Joy said.

"Your diary? What'd you bring it to school for?" Zach asked.

"Well, it's not exactly a diary. It's kind of a journal, but it's got private stuff in it."

"About me." Alan smirked.

"And I need it for projects because I wrote up all about Dancer in it. Oh, and Leeann, can you ride over again this afternoon? My father won't let me take Dancer out of the ring and ride him anywhere unless someone goes with me."

"Sorry," Leeann said. "I don't have a horse to use."

"Well, but what about Sassy?" Joy asked.

"I'm not allowed to borrow him anymore."

"Oh, Leeann!" Joy said. "That's rotten. It's so boring going round and round that ring. I want to go trail riding."

"I told you I'd go with you," Alan said.

"Oh, sure! You know it takes you forever to ride

71

from your house to mine. And anyway, Alan, you never do what you promise."

Without disputing that, Alan asked, "How about talking your father into letting you meet me halfway?"

Joy sighed. "He'll say no." Her voice rose to a wail. "What's the fun of having a horse if I can't ride it?"

Leeann was so disgusted at the fuss Joy was making that she said, "Joy, believe me, you don't know how lucky you are to own your own horse."

"Well, I don't feel lucky," Joy snapped. She grabbed the book Alan was still clutching and turned her back on the three of them. "See you later," she said and walked off toward the girls' room.

"She didn't ask *me* to ride with her," Zach complained.

"She's afraid one of your monsters might step on her precious palomino and squash it," Alan said.

Zach let go of him. Alan promptly shoved an elbow in his gut. Zach grunted. "Your girlfriend gets worked up pretty easily, Alan," he said.

"Yeah, well, she's used to getting her own way," Alan said. "She was born a year after her folks had Joey, so they think she's perfect. She is, compared to her brother."

Leeann suspected she was the one Joy was angry at because Joy ignored her all morning. Once in math class, Joy even turned away as if she hadn't heard when Leeann asked her what page they were supposed to be on in the math book. At lunchtime Leeann didn't know if she'd be welcome at the table where Joy was already sitting across from Alan and Zach. They hadn't left any room for her, and she couldn't tell whether they'd deliberately not saved the space, or couldn't find more in the crowded cafeteria.

She hesitated with her tray, regretting the loss of the first friends she'd made. Then she spotted Kristen waving at her. Kristen wasn't sitting with the group either but at the far end of a table of rowdy boys. Leeann took the seat across from her.

"Did you have fun at Joy's Saturday?" Kristen asked wistfully when Leeann was settled.

"Yeah, I did. Until afterwards. I got in trouble for borrowing a horse without permission and now I'm not allowed near any horse on the ranch."

"You took a horse? You did that? Wow!" Kirsten's eyes widened.

"Don't ask me why," Leeann said miserably. "I don't normally do stuff like that. Anyway, I should have known I'm not the type to get away with anything."

"Me neither," Kristen said. "I'm always getting in trouble, and I don't even do anything wrong. I mean, not like stealing a *horse*."

Leeann winced. "You're making me sound like an outlaw, Kristen."

"Well, I don't mean to. I mean, the stuff I get in

trouble for is just . . . like you know, not speaking in the right tone of voice or not looking grateful about something."

To have a grandmother like Kristen's would make life really miserable, Leeann thought.

They ate their lunches in companionable silence until Kristen said cheerfully, "I know what. You could stop over after school and meet Moley today. My house is back there behind the teachers' parking lot." She pointed at the window.

The whole town was visible past the parking lot. It consisted of a cluster of small houses, a church, a convenience store with gas pumps in front of it, an auto repair shop and a stop light.

"My mom would drive you home," Kristen said. "She never minds driving people places."

"I don't know about today," Leeann said because Rose expected her to come home on the bus. "Maybe tomorrow?"

"No." Kristen shook her sleek cap of dark hair sadly. "It has to be today. See, Grandma doesn't let me have friends over. She wants us to keep ourselves to ourselves. That's what she says. But today she's driving my grandpa to the doctor in Tucson and they won't be back until suppertime."

"Won't your mother let you have friends over, either?"

"Well, my mother does what Grandma says. See, we're living with my father's parents because my dad's working in Antarctica on a weather station.

Even my grandfather does what Grandma says. That's just how it is."

Sadness leaked from Kristen's every word. Leeann felt so sorry for her that she changed her mind. "I'd love to meet Moley," she said. After all, Kristen's gesture toward friendship shouldn't be rejected. Leeann could call the ranch and leave a message for her mother with whomever answered the phone.

There was no time allotted for projects that day. Ms. Morabita had a headache and told the class to read silently and not to talk. When a few students started chatting with each other anyway, she immediately slapped them down with detentions. A lot of notes were passed back and forth instead. Leeann thought Ms. Morabita might not excuse her to make a phone call in her bad mood, but the teacher readily gave her permission.

Mrs. Holden took the message for Rose. She sounded unfriendly. Leeann wondered if her horse thievery had turned Mrs. Holden against her, too. There must be something she could do to make the people at Lost River Ranch forgive her for borrowing Sassy. It would probably have to be something pretty spectacular. But what?

CHAPTER 8 ————————

Kristen's house, like other desert homes Leeann had seen, was as hidden as a well-wrapped box by the thick, roof-high adobe wall around it. Without inviting Leeann inside, Kristen hurried her past the house to the corral behind it. Leeann was shocked when she saw the swaybacked gray horse there, drooping like an unwatered plant outside a shed.

"Moley," Kristen sang out, "I'm home."

The animal didn't respond. His knobby-kneed legs barely seemed able to hold him upright. Kristen put her fingers to her lips and whistled piercingly. *That* made the horse look up. He roused himself enough to amble stiffly toward Kristen, who bent to slip through the rails of the corral. Leeann followed her.

Kristen put her arms around Moley's bony head and murmured endearments to him. In return he muttered softly. "He talks to me," Kristen said to Leeann. "We understand each other, Moley and me."

"He certainly knows you, Kristen," Leeann said.

76

It was the only positive comment she could honestly make about the horse.

"Yes. Moley loves me and I love him." Kristen's face was bright with pleasure as she stroked his neck.

Leeann wondered if Kristen realized how fragile Moley was. He appeared to have used up all but the husk of his life. Could he even see anymore out of those filmy eyes?

"Want to help me groom him?" Kristen asked.

"Sure." So long as Kristen didn't mean to ride the animal, Leeann was willing.

Moley perked up some as Kristen brushed and buffed his clean, mottled gray hide. His long black tail swished while Leeann combed his mane. "There," Kristen said with satisfaction when she'd finished and had hung a feed bag of oats over his head.

"Now would you like something to drink?" she asked Leeann. "Grandma says soda's bad for you, so we don't have any, but we have apple juice. Or I could make lemonade. And Mom usually bakes cookies on Mondays. That's the one day she doesn't work at the church."

"Apple juice sounds great," Leeann said.

The butter cookies had been left to cool in a pan on the counter in the small, neat kitchen. Beautifully shined copper-bottomed pots hung over the stove and small plants flourished on a stand near the window of the cheerful room.

"I like your house," Leeann was glad to be able to say. She could see the living room, which was smaller than the one Rose and she had had in Charlotte before Big John made them sell it. But it looked cool and comfortably furnished with a couch and chairs full of pillows.

"It's my grandparents' house," Kristen corrected her. "Someday, if my father changes his job, we might get a place of our own again. Meanwhile, I sleep with my mom and we try to keep out of the way."

"I sleep with my mother now, too," Leeann said, "in a really tiny cabin." She wondered if Kristen and her mother had an easier time of it than she had with Rose, who flung her warm body about at night and woke Leeann up with her groans. But she didn't know Kristen well enough to discuss something that intimate.

"Joy and Alan have their own rooms," Kristen said. "Their families are pretty rich. But Zach—his mother's been sick so long, and they're pretty poor. So Zach has to do the wash and the housework and stuff. I mean, I do housework too for my grandma. But he's a boy. Not that *that* matters, of course, but . . ." Kristen showed her dimples in a rueful smile, as if she'd been caught out in old fashioned male-chauvinism. "Anyway," she continued, "Grandma says scrubbing floors is good for your soul."

Leeann wrinkled her nose in disgust at that idea.

Kristen chuckled and confided with another play

of dimples, "When I grow up, I'm going to have a maid."

Leeann laughed. "A maid and a cook, and a horse of my own," she said.

"Well, I'm lucky. I already have my horse," Kristen said, "but I want a dog and some cats, too, and maybe a rabbit. I love animals."

"Me too." Leeann felt comfortable with Kristen, so comfortable that when they were eating cookies and drinking apple juice at the kitchen table, Leeann risked asking, "Kristen, do you ride Moley much?"

Kristen stiffened as if the question were barbed. "Not much. I'm too busy. I rode him yesterday around the corral. He's okay if I don't make him go very far. I think he's got arthritis or something." Her intense blue eyes sought Leeann's. "He's pretty old, you know."

"I guessed he was."

"But he's the sweetest horse in the world," Kristen said. "And he could live lots more years. Some horses live till they're over thirty. I read that in a magazine at the vet's office."

"You have a vet to treat Moley?"

"No. Grandma doesn't believe in doctors—not for people much either. But when Mom took me to Tucson for shopping, I went to a vet's office and asked her what I could do for Moley. She said just keep him comfortable, with lots of fresh straw to lie on and plenty of water, and give him oats once in a while."

Leeann nodded. She hoped for Kristen's sake that Moley survived for years.

"My father got Moley for me," Kristen said. "He used to have a horse when he was little. That's when Grandpa built the corral and the shed. So Dad said we might as well make use of it, since it was there."

They played Crazy Eights on the double bed in the bedroom Kristen shared with her mother. The room was neat and bare. Apparently mother and daughter put their clothes away, unlike Leeann and Rose, whose furniture was littered with garments clean enough to be worn again.

"My mother should be back by five," Kristen promised when she saw Leeann looking at the clock.

"If she's not, I'll call the ranch and ask Rose to send someone for me," Leeann said. She hoped Rose would be able to do that easily.

They talked about what kind of music they liked. Kristen preferred country and western, which she said was most of what was on the radio here.

"I like any kind of music that isn't too loud," Leeann said.

Kristen turned on her radio, and they played cards to the sounds of plaintive singers lamenting their lost loves.

"Have Alan and Joy been boyfriend and girlfriend for a long time?" Leeann asked.

"Forever. They always fit well together because they're both so rich and lucky and good looking."

"You're pretty, too, Kristen."

"No, I'm not. I look like a mouse. Anyway, that's what my grandmother says. She says I look like a little blue-eyed mouse."

"Maybe she means you're cute. Is Zach your boyfriend?"

"Zach? No way. Anyhow, my grandma would kill me if she thought I even looked at a boy. No, Moley'll do me until I grow up and get married and have a bunch of kids. Or I might become a vet and have a ranch with exotic animals like llamas and ostriches. I read about a place like that in California. I don't know if you can get rich from that, though."

Kristen didn't ask about Leeann, which was just as well, Leeann thought, because what could she say? She liked boys, some of them anyway, but none whom she'd liked had ever seemed to like her back. She hadn't even been kissed yet, except for a quick touch to her cheek once. It had happened during a kissing game in a dark closet at a party in Charlotte. The boy had been short and they'd bumped heads when Leeann bent down to allow his lips to reach her.

At the sound of a door shutting, Kristen whisked the cards back into their box and slipped it behind the headboard of the bed. "In case Grandma's come back first," she whispered in explanation. "Grandma doesn't approve of card playing."

Leeann wondered if the grandmother approved

of anything besides church going. She was glad when it turned out to be Kristen's mother who had come in. The woman was as small and sweet-faced as her daughter, but not as pretty.

"Of course, I'd be happy to drive Leeann home," she said as if she really were pleased to see Kristen with a new friend.

In the car on the way to Lost River Ranch, Kristen's mother asked Leeann how she felt about school and living on the ranch.

"I've always liked school. And I always wanted to live on a ranch," Leeann said, leaving out her disappointment in the one she'd come to.

"That's nice," Kristen's mother said. Hesitantly she asked, "Has your family joined a church here yet?"

"It's just my mother and me," Leeann said. She glanced at Kristen, who was in the back seat keeping them company on the drive. "And my mother's not much for church going." She saw Kristen wince and hurried to add, "Rose was Episcopalian, and so was my father. He used to go to church, I think."

"You call your mother by her first name?"

"I always have. I did it when I was little and my parents thought it was cute, so we just got in the habit."

"And your father? Was there a divorce?"

"No. He died of cancer. It took a long time." Six years out of her childhood. Leeann had added them up in a bitter mood once. "When Daddy was well enough, he used to take me out for breakfast while my mother slept in. It made me feel pretty special. I guess I was only three or four then."

"It must be hard, not having a father," Kristen's mother said sympathetically.

"Oh, I don't know. I've got a great mother," Leeann said.

"How nice to hear you say that!" Kristen's mother said.

"I've got a great mother, too," Kristen said. She snapped open her seat belt and leaned over her mother to give her a hug while she was driving.

"Careful," Kristen's mother said, but she was smiling.

"Thanks for driving me," Leeann said when she got out of the car in front of the ramada. "Maybe Kristen could come home with me tomorrow?"

"Oh, I don't know about tomorrow. We'll see." Kristen's mother smiled some more and said, "You be good now."

As the car pulled away, Kristen turned around in her seat and waved energetically out the back window at Leeann. Somehow Leeann had the feeling she wasn't going to see Kristen much outside of school, unless the grandmother started having to do extended errands more often. Or unless she and Kristen could figure out a way to get around both the grandmother and the distance between their homes.

CHAPTER 9 ---------------------------------

To Leeann's surprise, she found that she had a phone message from Joy waiting for her. "She left a number for you to call," Hanna said and gave Leeann a slip of paper.

Leeann used the telephone in the empty office. "Hi. How's it going with Dancer?" she asked when Joy answered.

"Not so good. He's not settling down at all," Joy said. "He wasn't this high strung when we bought him. Dad says maybe the guy had him on tranquilizers or something. Dad says we can make the guy take Dancer back if I want, but he's such a pretty horse. I mean, I'd really like him if he'd settle down."

"Yeah, I guess you'll just have to spend a lot of time with him and keep talking to him and stuff like that," Leeann said.

"Right, that's what I wanted to ask you. Dancer acted better when there were other horses around, and Dad said if you'd bring Sassy over, he'd pay you to ride my brother Joey around the ring."

"I can't, Joy. I told you that. I got into so much trouble for borrowing Sassy without permission that I'm not allowed near any horse on the ranch now."

"That rots," Joy said. "I mean, who am I going to get to ride with me?"

"Alan?"

"Oh, Alan's so unreliable, and he'd rather play his video games than ride, anyways."

"Well, Zach maybe."

"What, with those big old Percherons he's so proud of? Those aren't riding horses. They're work animals."

Leeann listened to Joy complaining for a while, then reminded herself that the problem was nothing she could help with. "Joy? Were you mad at me about something in school today?" Leeann interrupted to ask.

"I wasn't mad. Well, I was, sort of. Because you acted like I was making a fuss about nothing. But it's not nothing to me, Leeann."

"No, I guess not."

"Leeann, you *have* to ride with me," Joy said. "Maybe my dad can think of a way to get the Holdens to let you borrow a horse."

"It would be nice if he could," Leeann said, but she put down the receiver without hope. Joy was a moody girl. She'd been cold to Leeann in school all day, and then over the phone she'd talked as if they were already friends. It was hard to know how to take her. Of course, she did have a problem with

Dancer, but at least she had a beautiful young horse, and that was a lot more than Kristen or Leeann had.

"Rose," Leeann said when she found her mother rolling out pizza dough at the kitchen table, "I'm going to take my camera and go for a hike, okay?"

"Just stay on the trails, love, and be sure you know how to get back."

"And if I should happen to see a horse, I could take a picture of it from a distance, couldn't I?"

Rose laughed. "I can't imagine how Amos could object to that."

"Do you think he'll ever stop hating me and give me another chance?"

"Oh, Leeann!" Rose stopped rolling the dough and rubbed the back of a floury hand across her eye. "I'm so sorry, honey. If we weren't short on cash, I'd just quit and take us out of here this minute."

"You can't do that. Hanna needs you. I'm not complaining. It's just that I need to do my horse project for school, and I'm afraid I'll get in trouble somehow even just taking pictures of Sassy."

"If you do, I'll say I gave you my permission. But see you're back before seven. I don't want you roaming around in the dark."

"Love you," Leeann said, kissing her mother's round red cheek.

She was halfway out the door when Rose said, "You didn't tell me about your visit with Kristen, or anything about school."

"I will tonight. Right now I need to catch the

last of the daylight." Leeann ran for the cabin. Luckily she had a roll of film left in her camera.

Most of the horses were in the corral, but Sassy wasn't among them. Leeann skirted the fenced-in field and walked down to the wash without seeing any animal other than a single hawk riding a thermal on spread wings. The cloudless sky didn't look as if it could ever get dark, but she knew it would and quite suddenly.

She climbed the horse trail, stepping past mounds of dry manure and sending a lizard scuttling for safety under a small bush. Higher up, there was even less vegetation, but she could see farther, all the way to the bare rock hills that were shaped by wind and weather into a phalanx of mythological beasts. Shadows lay deep in the creases of their lumpy bodies. She'd need a horse to get as far as those hills. On foot she'd never make it even if she started early in the morning and walked all day.

A long-eared, angular rabbit that looked made of muscle hopped across a bare space between cactuses. Most plants here were armed to sting and prick. Leeann thought briefly of snakes and decided not to worry about them. They'd be more scared of her than she was of them, according to what she'd read. At the top of the next rise she looked back over the low roofs of the ranch house and its outbuildings and the barn and sheds, all the way back to town. Lights were just coming on like a sprinkle of fireflies in the distance.

Hoofbeats to her right made her turn. Amos was riding with a rope coiled at the ready toward a copse of trees in a gully. There was a stream at the bottom and Sassy was there, too, watching Amos coming toward him. Leeann raised her camera, but Sassy was too far away.

Quickly she slid down the other side of the hill. Chips of rock came with her in a clatter that caught Amos's attention. Since he was looking right at her, Leeann waved and said, "Hi. I'm hiking."

He didn't respond, but kept on the way he'd been going. Leeann hurried to get closer. Finally Sassy showed big enough in the camera's eye. Amos had gotten off his horse, which stood where he'd dropped the reins. He walked toward Sassy, who watched his approach alertly with ears turned forward. No sooner did Amos get close enough to slide a hackamore around Sassy's neck, than the horse sidestepped, dipped his head, brought it up and did something so unexpected it made Leeann laugh out loud.

Sassy stole Amos's hat! He took its brim between his big square teeth and flipped his head up so the hat came off Amos's head.

"Hey!" Amos yelled.

Before he could grab Sassy, the horse danced off into the stream. There he stood in knee-deep water with Amos's hat in his teeth and a glint in his eyes. The downward angle of Sassy's head and ears with that hat hanging from his teeth was pure mischief.

Leeann snapped shot after shot until she'd used up the rest of the film. If the pictures came out, they'd be hilarious.

Amos threw Leeann a killing look, but she was too amused to be scared. He waded into the stream with his boots on and tried to lasso Sassy, hat and all. As soon as the rope was in the air, so was Sassy. He reared up and then reared again. Not letting go of the hat, he looked back over his shoulder at Amos, who started yelling at him.

"You four-legged devil. Think you can play games with me, do you?" Amos ran forward and fell face down into the stream.

It wasn't funny anymore. Leeann was afraid Amos would hit Sassy if he caught him now. She set her camera down and dashed up the bank ahead of the horse. When she splashed into the stream, Sassy's head swung around to face her.

"Come on. You had your fun. Time to go back to the ranch now. Come on, sweetie, you don't want to run away from me," Leeann said.

Apparently Sassy didn't, because he stood still as Leeann came up to him and put her arm over his neck.

"How about giving me that hat, huh, you bad boy? It wouldn't look good on you anyway. Not your style. Let go, come on. Let go."

"Don't you get that hat ripped up," Amos called anxiously. He looked foolish standing in the stream with water dripping off him and a pale band of skin showing below his gray hair where the hat had hidden it from the sun.

Leeann kept stroking Sassy and talking. Finally he released the hat and Leeann caught it before it dropped into the stream. She brought it to Amos. "He was just teasing," Leeann said.

Amos blew out air in disgust just the way a horse did. His expression was unreadable as he took the hat, rubbed it off, and set it back on his head. "Paid a week's salary for this last winter."

"It's a nice hat," Leeann said. To her it looked like any other black felt cowboy hat, but she could see Amos took pride in it.

He didn't thank her for getting it back. He just nodded and stepped past her as he fashioned a temporary bridle out of his rope. The now-docile Sassy allowed Amos to fit it easily over his head.

Leeann waited until Amos had remounted and begun leading Sassy back toward the ranch. Then she picked up her camera and dragged herself after them on foot. It disappointed her that no matter what she did to help him, Amos refused to show any gratitude for it.

Half an hour before her seven P.M. curfew, Leeann got back to the kitchen. She sat down, chin on fist, to watch Rose cook.

"Tired?" her mother asked her.

"Discouraged," Leeann said. She related the hat incident. When she got to the part about Sassy in the stream with Amos's hat, Rose began to laugh, and Hanna, who had come in at the beginning of the story, hooted. Leeann burst out laughing with them and felt better afterward, even if nothing had changed and it still looked as if she'd remain horseless forever.

CHAPTER 10 ————————————

Leeann missed Kristen the day she didn't come to school. The sight of her cheek inches from her paper as she concentrated fiercely on her work had helped Leeann bring her own wandering mind back to task. Kristen's presence in class had been as comforting as the steady hum of a refrigerator in an empty house.

"Is Kristen sick or something?" Leeann asked the horse group at lunch.

"She must be dying," Zach said. "She's never yet missed a day of school."

"And you should know," Alan said, "because you're always here."

"Right, I don't take extra vacation days whenever I want, like some guys," Zach said.

"Listen, even the teachers take mental health days," Alan said.

"Just so they can sleep in?" Zach asked.

"Oh, stop it, you two," Joy said. She leaned forward and told Leeann, "One day Kristen came in with a fever of 103 and her mother had to come get her because she was too weak to walk home. Next day, she was right back in school."

That alarmed Leeann. She ate the chicken salad sandwich her mother had made her so fast that twenty-five minutes of the lunch hour were left. "I think I'll run over to Kristen's house and see what's wrong," she said.

"We're not allowed to leave school property," Joy warned her. "They call your folks if they catch you."

"My mother would understand," Leeann said.

"I'll go with you," Zach said. "We'll act like we're heading for the ball field and cut back to the parking lot from there."

"One kid's less likely to be seen than two," Leeann told him.

"And you know what they'll think if they catch you leaving together," Joy said.

"Woo, woo, woo!" Alan mocked. Zach's jaw tightened in embarrassment.

"Anyway, thanks for offering, Zach," Leeann said. She patted his shoulder on the way to the garbage can to dump her sandwich wrappings.

No one stopped her as she crossed the parking lot. She walked the short distance along the highway to Kristen's house and pulled the string on a bell hanging outside the wooden gate.

"Yes?" The large, stern-faced lady with artificial-looking black hair stared at Leeann suspiciously without opening the gate very far. Leeann had no doubt this was the grandmother.

"Um." Suddenly Leeann realized a phone call would have made more sense. What if the grandmother asked what Leeann was doing out of school? "Does Kristen want her homework for math?" Leeann improvised rapidly.

The grandmother frowned. "Kristen's in school. What about her homework?"

"Oh, ah, I thought . . . I thought she lost it," Leeann said. "Bye," she added and fled before the grandmother could uncover her flimsy deceit.

Where was Kristen? Leeann wondered if she'd run away from home. But she'd never leave Moley behind, and the horse was too rickety to go with her. Moley! It struck Leeann as she slipped into the now-empty cafeteria that Kristen might be with her horse. And by asking her ogre of a grandmother about her, Leeann could have roused the woman's suspicions and set her searching for her granddaughter. Leeann hoped she hadn't gotten her friend in trouble.

Impulsive. She was too impulsive. Rose said it was something she needed to work on, and it certainly was. It had already gotten her in trouble with Amos and Mr. Holden, and now it had possibly gotten Kristen in trouble as well. For the umpteenth time, Leeann made up her mind to think twice before she acted. But it was hard to break the habit of reacting too fast, especially when her feelings were involved.

Leeann fretted her way through the rest of the afternoon.

In the hall on the way to science class, Joy asked her what she'd found out at Kristen's house. Immediately Leeann confessed what she'd done.

"Tell you what," Joy said sympathetically. "I'll call her, and if her grandmother answers, I'll pretend I'm inviting Kristen to bring her horse over to my house."

"Thanks, Joy," Leeann said gratefully. "And would you call me as soon as you talk to her?"

"Sure," Joy said. "Oh, and Leeann, I meant to tell you. My dad's going to ask Mr. Holden about riding lessons for Joey. Mom said she'll bring Joey to the ranch if she has to. Ever since that time you got him on Sassy, Joey keeps talking about riding a horse. But he won't go near Dancer. He says he wants 'that girl's horse.'" Joy laughed as if she thought her brother's persistence was cute.

"Is Dancer calmer?"

"Not much. He shies away from me whenever I go near him. I'm going to start taking piano lessons so I won't have that much time to spend with him anymore. I wish I'd never picked that stupid horse."

"Maybe you should take him back to the person you bought him from."

"Yeah, but last night I told Dad I wanted to sell Dancer and get another horse and he got mad at me. He says I give up too easy. He wants me to keep trying to train Dancer. Some birthday present, huh?"

"I'd say it was," Leeann said. "Dancer's beautiful.

I'd be glad to work with him if he were mine." She shrugged. "I'd help you with him if we lived closer."

"Would you, Leeann? How about if you come to my house on the bus with me and then my mother could drive you home?"

"Maybe," Leeann said.

That evening she was called to the phone in the office. Without preamble, Joy said, "Kristen spent the day in the barn with Moley. He can't get up and he's breathing hard. Her grandmother didn't know she cut school because Kristen left the house like she was going to school, but she ducked out to the barn instead. Then she pretended to be coming home from school at the regular time and went to see Moley as usual. You won't believe what her grandmother said when Kristen told her Moley was down."

Leeann thought of the vertical lines dug deep as judgment between the grandmother's nose and lips. "What?" she asked.

"She said, 'Too bad. Sounds like he's had it.' Isn't that rotten? And she wouldn't call the vet or *anything*. And Kristen can't cut two days in a row or the office'll call home to find out why she's not in school."

"What can we do?" Leeann asked.

"I don't know. Kristen was crying so hard she could barely talk to me. She said she's not leaving Moley no matter what they do to her. She's spending the night with him."

After the phone call, Leeann found Rose and explained the situation to her. "Would you drive me to Kristen's house? I want to stay in the barn with her tonight so she won't be alone."

"Leeann, I can't do that without permission from Kristen's mother or grandmother. Suppose they found you there?"

"But Kristen shouldn't be alone with a dying horse, Rose."

Rose sighed. "All right then. We'll go over and talk to them."

"The grandmother's a witch," Leeann warned.

"Come on, Leeann, don't exaggerate. You don't really know the woman," Rose said.

Leeann was leaning on the front desk, waiting for her mother, when the phone call came in from Joy's father. She heard Mr. Holden talking to Mr. Childs as if the two of them were old friends.

"You don't say, Gordon. That boy of yours actually rode one of our horses? Well, I'll be! Sassy?" Mr. Holden's eyes found Leeann's over the desk. "Oh, yes, I know which one Sassy is. Well, the horse's steady enough once a rider's on his back, but keeping him in a corral's not so easy. Amos'd probably pay you to take that animal off his hands. Want a good horse cheap?"

Leeann held her breath. But Joy's father must have said one horse was enough to handle.

"Yes, I know," Mr. Holden said. "They're a big responsibility. Sure, you can bring the boy here to

97

ride. Well, I don't know." His eyes stayed fixed on Leeann. She stiffened.

"Oh, it's possible Leeann could handle the horse, but anyone can do that. It's catching Sassy that's the problem . . . okay, I'll put you down for two o'clock, and if Joey likes it, we'll make that a standing date. Fine. Glad you called."

Mr. Holden put down the receiver. He looked at Leeann and shrugged. "Too bad Amos is down on you. I'd have been glad to let you handle this. I doubt any of our wranglers'll be much good with a boy like him. If none of them work out, you may get your chance yet."

"I hope so. I mean, I'd really like to do it," Leeann said.

"Yes, your mother told me how you feel about horses. I'm sorry you got off on the wrong foot here, Leeann."

"Me too," she said.

Rose came out then. "Ready, Leeann?"

"Just a minute, and I will be." Leeann raced back to their cabin and grabbed a jacket, a blanket, and a pillow in case she was allowed to stay with Kristen. The car ride to Kristen's house only took twenty minutes. The grandmother came to the gate again. Even in jeans and a sweatshirt she was imposing.

"Kristen's gone to bed," she said when Rose explained that Leeann was a school friend of Kristen's and was concerned about her.

"But her horse—we understood the horse is sick," Rose said.

"It's an old horse and it's dying," the grandmother said stiffly. "We'll take care of it. No need for you or your daughter to worry." She was barely holding the gate ajar as if they might try to force their way in. And she hadn't once glanced at Leeann.

"Well," Rose said helplessly, "if there's anything we can do."

"Nothing, thank you." The woman put on a cardboard smile. "Nice of you to be so neighborly." She shut the gate without even waiting for them to turn away from it.

"She thinks we're busybodies," Rose said. "I'm sorry, Leeann. You may be right about her disposition. She's one tough lady."

A truck zoomed by on the road; its headlights slashed the darkness. When it was gone, only the halo of lights over the gas pumps and the golden seam of light leaking from the curtained windows of the house across from Kristen's remained to break the loneliness of the night.

"I bet Kristen's snuck out and is in the shed now," Leeann said.

"Maybe, honey, but we'd just get her in trouble if you went out there to see and got caught by her grandmother. The best we can do right now is to leave."

Zach called after Leeann returned to the ranch. "So how's Kristen making out?" he asked.

"I don't know." Leeann told him what the grandmother had said.

"Poor kid," Zach said. "That horse is like the only thing she ever talks about."

"Besides her grandmother."

"Yeah, besides the dragon lady."

The next morning Kristen walked into the classroom and went directly to her seat near the window. The corners of her mouth were turned down in mourning and her face was white. Leeann, Alan, and Zach were gathered around Joy's desk, but Kristen didn't even look their way.

"Kristen," Leeann called. "What happened?" She went to Kristen, followed by Joy. Kristen kept her eyes straight ahead.

"I wanted to stay with you last night," Leeann said. "My mother brought me to your house. Did your grandmother tell you?"

Kristen shook her head, her face expressionless. She didn't look at Leeann.

"Well, I was there. But your grandmother said . . . what happened, Kristen?" Leeann knelt down next to her and touched her arm. "Please tell me."

"They took Moley away. Grandma called a truck and they put Moley in a sling and took him away. I wanted to bury him next to the barn, but Grandma said we'd have to dig too big a hole." Silent tears coursed down Kristen's face. Leeann put her arms around her.

"Oh, Kristen, I'm so sorry. Your poor old horse," Joy said tearfully, and she, too, hugged Kristen. Meanwhile Zach and Alan hovered nearby.

"Sorry, Kristen," Zach said. "Moley was a great horse."

"Sorry, Kristen," Alan echoed.

The bell for homeroom rang. "We have to help Kristen to the girls' room. She's had a tragedy in her family," Joy announced dramatically when Ms. Morabita told them to take their seats. Ms. Morabita raised an eyebrow, but she let the three girls go without question.

Kristen had stopped crying by the time they got to the bathroom.

"I'll be all right," she said after she had washed her face. "We'd better get back to class."

Joy and Leeann looked at each other and Joy shrugged. Silently the three girls returned to English class.

Every time Leeann looked, tears were trickling down Kristen's cheeks as she doggedly worked on the vocabulary exercises they'd been assigned. It was only when they were walking to lunch together, following the other three, that Kristen burst out, "I hate my grandma. I just hate her. I wish she was the one who'd died."

"Moley was old," Leeann reminded her. "Your grandmother couldn't keep him from dying, Kristen."

"But she's so mean. She wouldn't let me stay

101

with him. She locked me in my room, and—oh, Leeann, he was my only friend." Her voice choked.

"Well, now you've got me," Leeann said. "I'm not as big as Moley, but at least I can talk."

Kristen laughed and gave a Leeann a grateful hug.

Joy insisted on buying Kristen lunch. Kristen thanked her and said she wasn't hungry. "Eat something," Joy said. "You'll feel better."

"Mother talk. You have that down pat," Alan said. "I could be dying and my mother would tell me to eat something."

"Always does make me feel better to eat," Zach said. He was, as usual, putting away twice as much food as any of them.

Kristen picked up the pizza Joy had bought her. "Thanks, Joy," she said, and ate the whole piece.

To cheer everybody up, Leeann told about how Sassy had stolen Amos's hat. "It was so funny I almost burst out laughing, but I was afraid he'd get mad, so I stifled it," she said.

"Wasn't he glad you got his hat back for him?" Alan asked.

"I don't think Amos has any glad in him," Leeann said.

Joy talked about how excited her little brother was that he was going to get a riding session on Sassy. "He wants 'that girl' to help him," Joy said. "That's what he calls you, Leeann, 'that girl.'"

"I wish I *could* help him," Leeann said, "but they won't let me."

"I heard about a riding program for disabled kids," Kristen said.

Eager to encourage Kristen's interest in something other than Moley's death, Leeann asked, "What about it?"

"Well, I don't remember much, except it's supposed to help their balance and stuff like that. It takes about three people to keep a kid on a horse, so they need a lot of volunteers to work it. Therapeutic Riding Program, that's what it's called."

"I'd be willing to volunteer for something like that," Leeann said.

"Me, too," Kristen said.

"Yeah, and me," Zach said.

"Just what you need, Joy," Alan said sarcastically, "another thing your mom can get into for Joey."

"Oh, I know I complain because my mom spends half her life at Joey's school, but . . ." Joy studied Kristen, who had finally stopped crying. Then she turned to the others and said, "I'll ask Mom if she knows about therapeutic riding. If we could all volunteer together, it might be fun." She raised her eyebrows and with a tilt of her head silently pointed out to Zach and Leeann that it would be good for Kristen to get involved.

So Joy was capable of concern about someone besides herself, Leeann noted, glad to regain her first impression of a friendly, warmhearted girl. They were a good bunch, these Arizona classmates, Leeann thought. She'd been really lucky to land in their midst.

CHAPTER 11 ————————————

The school bus dropped Leeann off at the ranch just in time to witness the disastrous finale of Joey's first riding session. Mrs. Childs was standing outside the corral wringing her hands. Joey was up on a mounting block struggling wildly with Amos, who was trying to get him onto the back of a small, barrel-shaped horse.

"No, no, no!" Joey screamed in terror.

"He wants Sassy," Mrs. Childs said to Amos. "Couldn't you get—"

"This here is the gentlest horse we got," Amos interrupted her. "This here is a mannerly horse." He turned to Joey and growled, "Now you sit quiet on her and she'll show you. Sit!"

But Joey wouldn't sit. As soon as Amos got him on the saddle, he shifted so that he was leaning precariously toward the mounting block. His cry of "No" became inarticulate yelling and thrashing about. Amos finally hoisted him off the horse and set him feet first on the ground. Instantly Joey crumpled onto his back in the dirt, wailing. Mrs.

Childs crouched beside him and drew him into her arms.

"What's he yelling for?" Amos asked indignantly. "I didn't hurt him."

"He came expecting to ride Sassy, and he's very disappointed," Mrs. Childs said in a voice like a block of ice.

"I told you. Sassy took off somewhere. And this here is a better horse anyways."

"You don't understand." Mrs. Childs gave Amos a glance of disdain while she sat Joey up. He clung to her, quiet now. "I'll bring Joey back tomorrow and we can try him on Sassy then," Mrs. Childs said.

"A kid like him don't belong on a horse," Amos told her.

"He'd do fine if someone had the patience to help him," Mrs. Childs snapped. "In any case, I'd like to see how he does on Sassy."

She looked up and saw Leeann, who had come halfway to the corral and stopped because she was leery of going near Amos. "Perhaps my daughter's friend, Leeann, could help Joey tomorrow. He trusts her," Mrs. Childs said.

Amos glanced sullenly at Leeann and said to Mrs. Childs, "You better see Mr. Holden about that." He led the barrel-shaped horse out of the corral and back toward the barn.

"I'm Leeann," Leeann introduced herself. "It's nice to meet you, Mrs. Childs."

"I guessed who you were," Mrs. Childs said with a grin. "You've made such a hit with everyone else in my family that I've been eager to meet you." She held out her hand and Leeann shook it.

"Hi, Joey," Leeann said then. "I'm sorry Sassy took off again, but how come you didn't like that nice horse Amos saddled up for you?"

Joey shuddered without lifting his head from his mother's shoulder or answering Leeann.

"He's exhausted," Mrs. Childs explained. "Come on, Joey, honey, we'll go home."

"Ride horsey," he whimpered.

"Not today, Joey. We'll come back tomorrow."

"Sassy's playing hide and seek with us today, Joey," Leeann said.

"Ride horsey," Joey insisted.

"Want me to go look for Sassy now, Mrs. Childs?" Leeann offered.

"No, thanks, Leeann. He's too tired to try again anyway." Lines showed around Mrs. Childs's lovely eyes when she smiled at Leeann. "But tomorrow I'll wait until you're home from school, and then I'd appreciate your seeing to it that the horse is available before I come. I'll call you."

"Well, I can tell you if he's around, but I'm not allowed to go near the horses, Mrs. Childs. Everybody here's mad at me because I borrowed Sassy without permission last weekend."

"Don't worry," Mrs. Childs said, as she got Joey to his feet. "I'll fix that."

Leeann supported Joey on one side while his mother held his arm on the other. Between them they walked Joey to Mrs. Childs's van and buckled him into his seat belt.

"Bye-bye," Joey said when his mother was seated behind the wheel and had turned on the engine. "Bye-bye, Girl. I love you."

Leeann laughed in surprise. "Thanks, Joey. I love you, too."

Mrs. Childs let out a sigh of relief. "Good. He's getting over his disappointment." She lowered her voice so that only Leeann could hear. "I'll tell you something," she said. "Even if Sassy had been here, that wrangler is the wrong person to handle a kid like Joey. I'll insist that you and Joy be allowed to help him ride—if that's okay with you."

"It would be wonderful, but I don't think Mr. Holden'll let me."

"Wanna bet?" Mrs. Childs twitched her lips and her eyes narrowed. Suddenly her prettiness showed a knife edge. "One thing I've learned from raising Joey is how to fight for what I want."

"Mrs. Childs," Leeann said impulsively, "did Joy tell you about that therapeutic riding program for kids?"

"Yes, I've already located the people in Tucson who do it. I'm going down there to see what's involved. Plenty of parents of special needs children around here would be interested. But I understand it will take lots of volunteers to run a program like that."

"Right, but I'd be willing, and so would Zach and Kristen. Probably Alan would be, too, if Joy does it." Leeann was thinking that since it was for a good cause, Kristen's grandmother might be persuaded to let her get involved in the program.

"Good," Mrs. Childs said. "I'd like to get started before Joey loses interest, even if we can't do things very professionally at first."

Leeann's hopes soared. She felt the way she did before Christmas when she didn't know what she would get but knew it would be good.

Rose had been off shopping for food supplies with Hanna. When the two women returned, Leeann helped them restock the refrigerator and pantry. The wranglers had the horses back in the corral by the time Leeann was finished, but she didn't see Sassy among them.

She followed skinny Robuck, who was carrying tack into the barn, and asked him about the horse.

"Still gone, and Amos said he don't care if that horse never comes back." Robuck grinned at her over his shoulder as if he thought that was funny. "He says that horse tried to wreck his good hat."

"Sassy was just teasing," Leeann said.

"Yeah, well, Amos don't much take to horses with a sense of humor," Robuck said.

Leeann did her math homework while Rose and Hanna made dinner for the guests. Later, she went out to check on Sassy again. It was hard to distinguish one horse from another in the dark, especially since so many had the characteristic brown body with black tail and mane of their sire, Darth Vader.

"Sassy," she called softly, standing at the railing of the corral, "Sassy." But none of the big bodies did more than shift from one foot to the other in the ten minutes she waited in the silky, cool evening air.

She didn't get really concerned until the next morning when Hanna told her Sassy was still missing.

"I'll look for him," Leeann said.

"You go to school. If he's not here when you get home, then you can go looking for him," Rose said.

In school that day Kristen seemed more aware of her surroundings, but she was obviously still very sad. At lunchtime, Joy reported that neglecting Dancer had served to improve her horse's disposition.

"He actually let me get on and ride him around the ring last night without giving me a hard time," Joy said. "My father says if he does that a couple more times, he'll let me take him trail riding—so long as someone goes with me."

"I'll go with you," Alan said. "We could ride to Wolf Canyon."

"Um, maybe," Joy said.

"I know a canyon back of Lost River Ranch I'd like to see again," Zach said. "My dad took me there when I was a little guy. How about I borrow the Percherons and you ride up there with me tomorrow, Leeann?"

Tomorrow was Saturday.

"If Sassy's not back when I get home from school, I'm going to search for him on foot. But if he's still not back tomorrow, it would be great to go looking for him on horseback," Leeann said. "Maybe if we ride toward your canyon we'll find him, Zach."

"Could be," Zach said with a smile that lifted his long jaw.

"You're really willing to ride those monsters?" Alan asked Leeann. "You'll be sore for a week just getting your legs around them."

"They'll get me farther than my own two legs," Leeann said.

"Amos *has* to lend you a horse to go looking for Sassy," Joy said.

"Why? He has it in for Sassy and me both," Leeann said. "Amos wouldn't do anything for either of us." She laughed. "And Joey's riding experience didn't make Amos like us any better."

"Mom said things didn't work out, but she didn't want to talk about it. What happened?" Joy asked.

Leeann described how Amos had behaved with Joey. "Incidentally, I told Mrs. Childs you'd all be willing to volunteer if she gets a therapeutic riding program going here." Leeann looked at Zach.

"Sure, so long as it doesn't interfere with my chores," he said.

"I'll help if my grandmother lets me," Kristen said.

"What are you going to do this weekend?" Leeann asked her.

"I don't know. Clean my room and read, I guess."

"I thought your grandmother wouldn't let you read anything but the Bible," Alan said.

Kristen frowned at him. "She's not *that* bad."

As they were depositing their garbage in the cans, Zach said quietly to Leeann, "I was thinking. It'd be easier if we both rode one horse. I mean, they aren't really riding horses and handling them might be tough for you."

Alan, who had been standing close enough behind them to hear, teased, "Ooo hoo hoo, sexy!"

Zach threw him a disgusted look that didn't shake Alan's grin.

"Come on, Alan," Joy said. "We're going to be late for math." She winked over her shoulder at Leeann as she hustled Alan off.

Sassy was still missing when Leeann got home from school. "Does he usually disappear for this long?" she asked Hanna.

"Never that I've heard," Hanna said. "Holden's after Amos to get him back. Poor Amos had to ride out to look for him before he did his chores. You should have heard him cussing." Hanna laughed.

Leeann didn't think it was funny. What if Sassy

was in trouble, trapped somewhere, or hurt? She hiked around the ranch for more than an hour, covering five or six miles, and returned in time for dinner without seeing anything but a roadrunner and a bird she couldn't identify.

Rose gave her permission to go searching with Zach on Saturday, and Leeann called him to ask him to come over early. "I'll bring a picnic lunch," she said.

"My mouth's watering already," Zach said.

After breakfast Saturday morning, Rose offered cold roast chicken, fruit, and nutcake for the lunch. In addition, Leeann made up a few peanut butter sandwiches in case Zach's appetite still needed satisfying.

"I want you home before suppertime, Leeann," Rose said. "And be careful."

"Aren't I always?" Leeann asked.

"Not when your feelings are involved," her mother said, but she took the edge off her criticism with a hug.

Leeann dressed in old jeans, a T-shirt, and the sport boots she used for riding. She borrowed one of Rose's straw hats and tied a jacket around her waist just in case. Then she filled up a couple of gallon jugs of water and tied them together with a rope long enough to go over a Percheron's wide back.

When Zach rode up on Paul, his favorite of the two massive horses, Leeann was waiting for him on the ramada with the lunch in a backpack and the water jugs beside her. She even had a carrot for Paul, who dipped his big white head and took it gently from her fingers. A quiet strength pulsed from his shoulder as she leaned against him while Zach dismounted and arranged the water bottles. He also had brought water, she noticed. And extending from behind the saddle was a blanket where a second person could sit.

"We can trade off sitting in the saddle," Zach said. "Some places we'll both have to walk anyway. Pop drew me a map of how to get to the canyon. It's got like a keyhole pass into it that's pretty narrow. Paul may not fit through. See, last time we were there Dad had a couple of little cow ponies."

"Sounds exciting," Leeann said, "but I hope we find Sassy before we get to your canyon."

"Yeah, but you know, this canyon's a really special place, Leeann. I didn't want to say it in front of the others because Pop says the less people know about it the better. That canyon's got petroglyphs that are over five hundred years old."

She must have looked puzzled because he explained, "Petroglyphs. You know, those rock paintings of animals and stuff that ancient Indians made? We've got a lot of them around here, but kids go and mess them up with graffiti or they just get worn out from too much traffic and exposure. Some people actually blast out the rocks and take them home for a souvenir."

"They sound interesting, Zach, but to be honest, what I really want most is to find Sassy."

He nodded, and Leeann asked how long it was since he'd been to the canyon.

"Years. It was back when Ma wasn't so bad we couldn't leave her alone. My pop and me used to go camping weekends. He didn't work so hard then." Zach stopped to think about it. Then he said wonderingly, "He used to laugh a lot and be the best company." He shook his head.

"Well, come on, you get up first." Zach made a basket of his hands. Leeann stepped into it and vaulted lightly onto Paul's dappled rump, grabbing hold of the back of the saddle.

She thought about Kristen home under her grandmother's prison rules and felt sorry for her. It was fun to be riding out with Zach. It would be even better if they came riding back with Sassy.

CHAPTER 12 —————————————

Once Paul started walking, the rocking motion thrust Leeann's body against Zach's. Suddenly the parts of her touching his bony back sprouted sensitive new nerve endings. It was both pleasant and scary to find herself tingling wherever she touched him.

The tingling kept her from paying much attention to the Lost River Ranch horses, which were grazing freely again on their day off. The one thing she did note was that Sassy wasn't among them. The solid Percheron rocked his passengers along rhythmically past the bunkhouse where Amos and his wranglers slept.

Amos's voice preceded him from the dark of the open doorway. "Where you headed?"

"Ho," Zach commanded Paul, who stopped and stood as if he'd never budge again. Politely, Zach answered, "You know that butte that looks like a horse's head?"

"Up west of here a few miles?" Amos asked.

"Yeah. My dad took me camping in the canyon

116

back of that once. That's where I'm taking Leeann."

"You better not mess with the petroglyphs there," Amos warned. "They're the property of Lost River Ranch."

"We're just going to look," Zach said mildly.

Amos grunted, and then spoke to Zach as if Leeann weren't there. "We got a horse missing. If you should happen on it and could bring it back, I'd be obliged."

"We're planning to look for Sassy," Zach said.

Finally Amos slid his eyes at Leeann. "You want a saddle and bridle in case you happen onto him?" he asked Zach.

"That'd be great," Zach said.

"Wait a minute."

"Could be he's easing up on you, Leeann," Zach said as Amos disappeared.

"You maybe, not me. He hasn't said a word to me."

Zach sniffed and rubbed his nose. "He's talking to you through me."

Amos reappeared with a small worn saddle and bridle in hand. "Should fit the girl, skinny as she is," he mumbled and handed the gear up to Zach. He rearranged the water jugs so that they balanced out the weight of the saddle hanging on the other side of Paul.

"If you come upon the horse and it's in trouble, you get on back here and let me take care of it," Amos said.

"You think something's happened to Sassy?" Zach asked.

Amos shrugged. "He's never missed a feeding before." His eyes reached for Leeann as if he wanted to say something. But then he didn't.

She sensed the right words now might ease the bad feelings between them, but none came to her. Instead Zach started Paul up and they plodded on their way.

"Be careful now," Amos called after them.

By the time they'd seesawed their way past the hill where Amos most often led the trail riders, the sun was heavy on their backs. Leeann was getting used to the feel of Zach's body as she bumped into him going downhill or grabbed hold of him to keep from sliding off Paul going uphill. They came to the first dried-up riverbed and stopped in the shade of cottonwood trees along its bank.

"Stretch time," Zach said. He slid off the saddle and reached up to help Leeann off. It was so far down, she took his hands and let him break her fall as she jumped. "Not exactly easy riding, is it?" Zach asked her.

"No, but it's fun. This was a great idea, Zach."

"Want to do the driving for a while?"

"No, thanks. I'm fine." She wasn't. The blanket was chafing her legs, but she thought that since this whole operation was for her sake, she should be the one to suffer.

They followed the sandy bed of the river for a

half a mile or so, walking and leading Paul, who sank in up to his hocks in soft patches. Then Zach led them up the bank on rocks that had fallen from a wind-sculptured bluff. Its tan rock face had eroded into long curving shapes like the headless bodies of giants. The horse seemed uneasy on the loose boulders, and Zach had to coax him along.

"I don't know," Zach said. "The canyon's farther than I remembered. I guess when my father rode me up there on the cow ponies, the going was easier. Peter and Paul are meant for pulling, not climbing."

"Should we turn around?" Leeann asked. She didn't want to, but she didn't want to harm Paul either.

"If we don't see the canyon once we get around this butte, maybe we'd better start back," Zach said. "It's a long way."

But when they got around the butte, there was just one more little hill to get around and then another and another until finally, they saw the horsehead-shaped formation Zach was looking for. "It's maybe another mile," he said, "but it should be easy riding. Looks like there's nothing but plain old mesquite and creosote bush from here to there. Let's stop and have lunch."

A snake slid out from behind the rock Leeann had picked to sit on and she jumped back.

"Yeah, rocks aren't too good an idea around

119

here. They're shelters for snakes and scorpions, not to mention lizards." Zach took the blanket off Paul's back and spread it on the ground for her. Leeann laid out the lunch, glad to be off the Percheron for a while.

The chicken made Zach's eyes brighten. "A feast!" he said, rubbing his hands together and looking so carnivorous she laughed.

She left most of the chicken for him. Water was what she needed to satisfy her. The peanut butter sandwiches were so dry and sticky, she only ate half of one. Instead she had two peaches.

Zach ate heartily of everything. "Great lunch," he said, licking the cake frosting off his fingers. "I can see why your mom got hired to cook."

"Oh, she's not a professional cook. She's just learning. But Rose can do anything, except paperwork, which she hates."

"My mother used to work in an office," Zach said. He stretched out his arms and cracked his knuckles. "I don't remember those years too well, except that my dad seemed young then. He acted like a kid most of the time. You lost your father, Kristen said."

"Yes. He died of bone cancer when I was almost nine."

"That must have been hard for you," Zach said.

It had been. She remembered her ninth birthday as the worst of her life, not so much because she missed her father as because her mother had been so sad. "It must be hard for *you* now, Zach, taking care of your mother."

"No, we've got it down to a science, Pop and me. And the lady from the county health department helps a lot. The only thing is it keeps getting worse. Like now she's hardly talking. I mean, she tries, but—" He swallowed and then went on. "About all she does is watch TV. It's sad. I mean, to think about how it is for her. I talk to her, tell her stuff about my day . . . like, she knows about you."

"She does?"

"Yeah." He looked embarrassed. "I told her you were my girlfriend. I thought she'd get a kick out of that. See, Pop teases me that no girl's going to want an ugly mutt like me."

"You're not an ugly mutt," Leeann protested loyally. "Why does he say a thing like that?"

"Because, you know, he was a good-looking guy. Still is. But he doesn't say it to be mean. I guess he thinks I don't care about how I look."

"Alan's handsome, but I'd pick you over him anytime," Leeann said.

"You would?" Zach's eyes glowed with pleasure. Then he swallowed hard.

"Leeann," he began, and hesitated. She could tell he was going to ask her for something, and she tensed because she wasn't ready to give him anything like a kiss or the promise that she'd go steady with him.

"I feel so sorry for Kristen," she said quickly. "I wonder how long she's going to go on mourning Moley."

Zach sat back on his heels abruptly, as if he were aware that she had put him off. "Don't know," he said.

"I wish Kristen's father would come back," Leeann said. "Maybe he'd get her another horse."

"Not while that grandmother's running things," Zach said. "She's a real fruitcake. She came into school last year with a list of books. The librarian thought she was just taking them out to read or something, but that old lady burned them, right in front of her own house, with a sign saying something like, 'Protecting young minds is our moral duty.'"

Paul shuddered and stomped his foot. Instantly, Zach turned his attention to his horse. When nothing seemed to be wrong, he continued, "Yeah, so then the school called the sheriff's office, and I guess they spoke to Kristen's grandma, but she never went to jail or anything. I don't even know if she paid for the books."

"And Kristen's mother's religious, too?" Leeann asked.

"Not like the grandmother. Kristen's mother's just normal religious. She does a lot of church work. But she's not, you know, going to pound her beliefs into everybody else."

"It's funny," Leeann mused. "I've only been here

a little while, but I feel as if I know you guys so well. It's wonderful to talk things over with someone who'll listen. I missed that back in Charlotte after my friends moved away. I'm glad you're helping me look for Sassy, Zach." She smiled at him, hoping she hadn't said too much.

Zach smiled back. His jaw didn't seem too long anymore. In fact, his homeliness had become appealing. She stood up. "Come on," she said. "We'll never get there and back in time if we don't move it."

"Okay, let's go," he said. They remounted Paul, who was able to go more quickly now that the ground was harder, although his "more quickly" was still plodding.

"Can Percherons gallop?" Leeann asked into Zach's ear.

He laughed. "Not if they can help it. Slow and steady is their pace."

The horsehead shape at the top of the butte got closer and closer until Leeann finally saw the cleft in the hill where the canyon was. She wondered if Sassy could possibly have come this far. After all, a horse couldn't disappear into thin air. He had to be somewhere past where Amos had looked for him, unless he'd been stolen. That was possible; someone could have found Sassy wandering and just led him off.

The entrance to the canyon looked like a giant keyhole in the rock. It was, as Zach had said, so narrow Paul could barely fit through it even after they dismounted. In fact, the horse resisted being led between the rock sides. Zach kept encouraging him, "Paul, step up. Step up," but the Percheron didn't move.

Leeann was so absorbed in the operation that she was taken by surprise by a whinny from inside the canyon. There on the far end, where a ribbon of water was falling onto flat rocks before disappearing into the sand, stood a horse.

"Sassy!" Leeann yelled. She ran to where Sassy was standing—awkwardly, with one leg stretched out—near a dishpan-sized pool of water. The horse was shivering and he didn't look well. It took only a glance to discover his hoof was wedged in a crevice in the rocks where a fallen boulder lipped over the space.

"That's why you didn't come home. You couldn't," Leeann said to Sassy as she hugged his neck.

Zach stepped up beside her. He'd left Paul stuck in the entryway with just his head in the canyon. Paul snorted. Sassy answered. Zach knelt next to the hoof and tried to feel down under it and tug up. "It's wedged in pretty good," he said.

"Zach, why don't you go back to the ranch on Paul and get Amos while I stay here with Sassy?" Leeann said.

"We should ride back together. Sassy's not going anywhere. Amos can come up tomorrow and chip away the rock or something."

"I'm not leaving him alone here," Leeann said flatly.

Zach looked at her and sighed. "Okay, maybe we can lift the boulder off so he can pull the hoof out himself."

Leeann crouched and tried to heave up the boulder. Zach laughed. "You can't budge that," he said. "Neither can I. We could try to rope Paul to this rock and then back him out of the canyon maybe."

They stripped everything but the bridle off the Percheron. Zach had a length of rope tied to the saddle bag and they also had the bridle and reins from the saddle Amos had lent Leeann. It was Leeann's idea to fit the extra bridle around the boulder, tie it to the rope, and tie the rope to Paul's reins.

"This is never going to work. It won't hold when he starts pulling," Zach said. And he was right. "Back step," Zach ordered his horse, who promptly obeyed. As soon as the Percheron moved back, the metal ring connecting the reins to the bridle opened. Once again Zach tried to talk his horse into coming all the way into the canyon.

Meanwhile, Leeann stroked Sassy, who seemed to take comfort from her attentions. He kept giving her gentle nudges with his head and nickering softly.

"At least you got stuck where there was plenty of water, didn't you?" Leeann told him. "And we'll get you out. Even if Zach has to go and get Amos to help, we'll get you out. And then you can have a big bucket of oats. You're hungry, aren't you, Sassy? I bet you are." There was no vegetation within reach. "Too bad we didn't save some of the lunch. Unless you want a peanut butter sandwich." Leeann offered him one. Sassy chomped at it and then looked foolish trying to lick the peanut butter off his teeth with his thick, clumsy tongue. Leeann laughed at him.

Zach called, "Leeann, I can't convince this critter to come in. He's probably scared he won't ever get out. We've got to leave Sassy here and go for help."

"Fine. You go. I'm staying."

"No. No way. It'll get cold and dark in a couple of hours. You've got to come with me."

It was while they were arguing that Paul suddenly shoved his broad body through the narrow entrance into the canyon. Once he was in, he stood there swishing his white tail over his dappled haunches and huffing as if he were still scared.

"Okay, feller. Now you do what you're built for," Zach said. He slung the rope around the boulder and tied the ends into a loop which he fitted around Paul's neck. It wasn't possible to turn the animal around in the narrow canyon. "Paul, back step," Zach ordered. "Back step."

Leeann yelled when the boulder flipped up and over. She was scared it would fall against Sassy, but it didn't. Immediately, she reached down the horse's slim leg and under the horny hoof to try

126

tilting the rock. "If I could just get it sideways . . ." she said.

"Let me try." Zach knelt beside her. His big hands were already knotty with a man's strength. Sassy was muttering anxiously and his side felt hot as he leaned against Leeann, but in a minute his hoof came free.

"There we go," Zach said.

Leeann hugged him and then she hugged Sassy, who was tossing his head as if he relished his newfound freedom. "Now let's get out of here and go home," Leeann said.

"The petroglyphs are up that way," Zach said regretfully. He was pointing at a cave opening halfway up the canyon wall. There would be a steep climb over a pile of fallen rocks to reach it.

"We can come back to see them next week," Leeann said. She was tired and anxious to get Sassy home to be fed and cared for. "Anyway, we still have to get Paul out of here."

"Yeah, you're right." Zach looked at his horse with concern. "Oh, boy, this isn't going to be easy." But Paul was more cooperative at backing out of the canyon than he'd been at squeezing into it. When the horse felt the stone girdle closing around his ribcage again, he didn't panic but backed out steadily at Zach's command. Sassy came through headfirst with ease. He'd thinned down some in the two days he'd been gone from the ranch.

"Do you think Paul could carry us both home?"

Leeann asked when Zach had resaddled him. "I don't know if Sassy's feeling up to taking me."

"Listen, you're a lightweight for him. It'll go a lot faster if you ride him," Zach said.

Sassy was busy eating leaves off a bush. Leeann saddled him and mounted. She pressed her heels into his side, and after some persuasion to get him to forsake the bush, they got underway.

"What do they look like?" Leeann asked Zach, who was so high up ahead of her on Paul, she felt as if she were riding a pony. "The petroglyphs?"

"Pictures of deer and sort of stick figures of men and the sun. The deer are the best."

"I'll bring my camera when we come back," she said.

"You really will go back with me?"

"Sure I will," Leeann said. "I want to."

"Next Saturday?"

"Fine," she said.

Would he kiss her in the cave in front of the petroglyphs? She thought he might. She thought she might even encourage him to try. She'd never enjoyed any boy's company as much as she enjoyed Zach's, and he was solid. He had a strength of character that had begun to seem beautiful to her.

CHAPTER 13 ––––––––––––––––––––

They were so late getting back to the ranch that on the last hill they saw Amos and Mr. Holden riding toward them against the backdrop of a pink and purple sunset.

"You found Sassy!" Mr. Holden said. "I thought sure that horse was a goner. Where was he?"

"Stuck in the canyon with the petroglyphs," Zach said. He added proudly, "Paul here pulled off a boulder that was trapping his hoof."

"You don't say! Well, I owe you for saving my animal's life. What can I do for you?"

Without hesitation Zach said, "Leeann helped as much as Paul and me. How about letting her ride Sassy whenever she wants?" He looked at Amos. Everyone looked at Amos. He was sitting on his horse in unsmiling silence, his lumpy face as forbidding as a desperado's on a wanted poster.

"That agreeable with you, Amos?" Mr. Holden asked.

The head wrangler shrugged. "The girl can do

what she wants so long as I don't have to chase that blamed horse no more."

"Fine," Mr. Holden said. He smiled broadly at Leeann. "Looks like anytime you can catch him, you can ride him, Leeann—unless Amos needs him for one of the guests. Now you and I have another matter to talk about."

"What?" Leeann held her breath, hoping her sudden good fortune wasn't about to reverse itself.

"Enid Childs is coming tonight to discuss a riding program for disabled kids that she wants to start here on the ranch. Says you and your friends will help her with it."

"Yes. Five of us want to volunteer, including me," Leeann said eagerly.

"Well," Mr. Holden cleared his throat as if he were uncomfortable. "The thing is, Amos doesn't want any part of the program, so I don't see it working out too well." Again all eyes went to Amos, who gave nothing back.

"On the other hand," Mr. Holden continued, "it's hard for me to say no to the Childses. Gordon Childs's daddy was my best friend. I know you've got to be tired, Leeann, but I'd appreciate if you would sit in to hear what Enid's got to say."

"I'd be glad to." Leeann was relieved that that was all he wanted.

"Any chance you can stay for supper and join us at the meeting, Zach?" Mr. Holden asked.

"Thanks, I can't. Pop expected me home long

since. Leeann'll keep me posted." He waved and thanked Mr. Holden again as he set off for home.

The meeting was in the library. Leeann was impressed at the way Joy's mother presided. She stood in front of the fireplace facing Mr. Holden, Amos, Leeann, and Hanna, all of whom were sunk deep into the cushioned leather couches lined up on three sides of the Navajo area rug.

"It's good of you to be here," Mrs. Childs began, "because I'm sure you're tired after your hard workdays. Well, I promise not to keep you long. I'll just tell you what I learned in Tucson, where they've got this Therapeutic Riding Program going. Apparently it's being done all over the country. Heaven knows how I missed hearing about it, but I'm delighted that, thanks to Leeann and her friends, I'm aware of it now."

She beamed at her audience and continued enthusiastically, "This program gives special-needs kids, kids who are physically or mentally impaired, experiences to make them stretch and grow."

From a large handwritten chart, she began reading aloud to them the benefits of assisted horseback riding. "First, sitting on a powerful animal and controlling its movements makes a child *feel* powerful. Just being up on a horse's back is a unique experience for a lot of kids who are used to looking up at the world from wheelchairs." Mrs. Childs glanced at each of them in turn to make sure she had their attention. "And special-needs kids who walk have to look up, too, because they tend to be small," she said.

Her second point was that riding stretches and exercises the muscles needed in walking because it simulates walking. It educates disabled children's muscles.

"Three," Mrs. Childs read aloud. "It teaches coordination. Many of these children have trouble learning their left from their right, and by directing a horse which way to go, they get a sense of it themselves."

Amos was sitting with his arms folded across his chest and his lower lip rolled out. Leeann saw his eyelids fall shut. Mrs. Childs looked his way, but she pushed on determinedly, "Four. There's a natural bond between a horse and a child who grooms and rides it. Some children who can't connect with people will connect with their horses. A child who can't even talk may learn to use voice commands with a horse."

She took a deep breath and smiled at her audience as she read the last item, which seemed to move her particularly, "Five," she said so fervently that Amos opened his eyes and straightened in his chair. "A child who is riding a horse is doing something special and privileged, and our children don't do much that makes them feel that way."

There were tears in her eyes as she concluded, "Now, I've already got a list of interested parents from the Bow Lane School for Special-Needs Children. These folks are enthusiastic about having their kids in this program and are willing to pay the costs for the special equipment."

"What special equipment?" Mr. Holden asked.

"Oh, like riding helmets or bike helmets approved for riding. Possibly some kind of braces. Things like extra mounting blocks, maybe one with a ramp for wheelchair-bound kids."

"You're going to put kids in a wheelchair on horseback?" Mr. Holden sounded alarmed. "How are you going to keep them from falling off?"

"Well, I was getting to that. You see, we'll need a lot of volunteers, because not only does the child need help mounting, but there should be a sidewalker on either side of the horse and someone leading the horse. Of course, the child's parent can be one sidewalker, but then Joy or Leeann or one of their friends can be the other. And if we could get a wrangler to lead the horse . . ."

"My boys already got enough to do," Amos objected. "There's no way we can free up cowboys for this." He turned to Mr. Holden and growled, "This is a guest ranch. We're not going into the business of renting out horses by the hour, are we?"

"No, of course not," Mr. Holden assured him.

"I'm willing to lead a horse around for a couple of hours a week," Hanna put in. "It sounds like a worthwhile use of free time to me."

"Actually," Enid Childs assured them, "half an

hour on the horse is about all these kids have the energy for. Say they come for an hour. Half that time will be spent getting the child used to the horse and grooming it. They might also help with the saddling up where that's possible."

"The thing is," Mr. Holden said, "it sounds dangerous to me. I mean, take a child in a wheelchair and put him on a horse when he doesn't have any muscle control?"

"The parents are all willing to sign releases so that anything that happens won't be your responsibility," Mrs. Childs said. "And if it makes you more comfortable, we can start with kids who can walk, like Joey. How about if we start with just three kids this week and see how it goes?"

"Three kids—that's nine people," Hanna said. "Who's your nine?"

"Well, you and Mr. Holden, the three parents, and four of the seventh graders."

"What about the horses?" Amos asked.

"Right, Amos," Mrs. Childs said. "That's where I desperately need your help. Would you be willing to pick horses out for us that are gentle and steady? Intelligent animals that respond well to people?"

Amos snorted. "Right, and then what do I tell the paying guests? Sorry, your favorite's being used by some kid that's got no business on a horse in the first place?"

Enid Childs's eyes turned sharp as drill bits.

"How do you determine who deserves to get the best horse, Amos?" she asked.

He fumed and avoided answering by turning to Mr. Holden. "It's time I turned in. I got to get up at five A.M. like usual."

"Right, Amos," Mr. Holden said. "You go on. Thanks for coming in to hear Mrs. Childs's presentation. And don't worry. I'm not about to pile additional work on you."

Amos harumphed and huffed his way out of the room.

"But if it's only one hour a week," Leeann said to Mr. Holden, "couldn't it be a time when the guests are eating lunch or something? Or a Saturday? I mean, the volunteers could saddle the horses and show the kids how to groom them and stuff like that."

"I hear you, Leeann," Mr. Holden said. He sighed. "All right. What we'll do is start this program without Amos. I suspect he may cooperate once he sees it working. That's if it does work."

"It will work," Mrs. Childs said with authority.

"Well, we'll see, won't we?" Mr. Holden said.

"And if it doesn't go smoothly right at first, you'll give us a fair chance?" she asked.

"We'll give you a couple of tries to get it rolling," he said. "How about Thursdays at four? That's the day the guests take all-day trips. They get back by mid-afternoon, and we don't offer late afternoon rides that day."

"And you'll pick three easy horses for us?" Mrs. Childs asked him.

"I'll pick them and help with what tack to use, and Hanna can supervise the volunteers."

"I'm sure I can find a few parents who know horses well enough to lead them around the ring," Mrs. Childs said. "Thanks, Holdy, you're a brick."

"Holdy!" He laughed. "Your husband tell you I used to be called that?"

"My father-in-law did before he died," she said.

Mr. Holden chuckled and nodded to himself. "Well, I suppose it's worth a try, anyhow."

Before she left, Mrs. Childs arranged with Leeann to convene a meeting of the volunteer seventh graders at lunch the next day. "I'll come in and talk to them about their responsibilities," Mrs. Childs said.

Leeann immediately called Kristen. "If your grandma won't give you permission, maybe Mrs. Childs can talk her into it," Leeann said. She'd begun to think Joy's mother was capable of talking people into anything.

"I'll tell Grandma it's helping the less fortunate like she always says is our duty," Kristen said. "That should get her." She sounded excited.

CHAPTER 14 --------------

Leeann wasn't sure Kristen would succeed until she came into homeroom on Wednesday with her dimples showing in a big smile.

"Grandma says okay, and my mother says she'll help out, too, if they need her."

"Maybe she could drive Zach and Alan home from the ranch on Thursdays," Leeann suggested.

"Oh, she'd be willing to do that for sure," Kristen said with another flash of dimples.

One last detail bothered Leeann. How could she be sure Sassy was available on Thursdays when Joey needed him? On the chance that he might be willing to give her the benefit of his experience without biting her head off, Leeann waylaid Amos on the way to the barn after school Wednesday and asked him what she could do.

"Only way is stow the horse in the barn after he gets fed in the morning. Or hobble him all day," Amos said.

"Sassy wouldn't like being hobbled," Leeann said. "I guess I better stow him in the barn. Thanks, Amos."

Thursday morning before she left for school, Leeann put Sassy in the barn in an empty stall. When she got home from school, though, Sassy had been taken out on an all-day trail ride with the rest of the favored horses. Leeann fretted until she saw Amos returning.

"He'll be in the barn when you want him," he said before she could ask him about Sassy.

Mrs. Childs hadn't yet arrived when Leeann saw a van marked Bow Lane School parking beside the barn. Apprehension overcame her. She didn't know anything about special-needs kids. She'd never been near any except for Joey, and just because he liked her didn't mean another child would. What if she couldn't handle this? Fear made a lump in her chest.

Joey was the first child off the van. He came running out waving his arms in the air excitedly. "Hi, hi, hi," he cried when he saw Leeann. He ran up to her and hugged her. "Where my horse?" he asked.

"We'll bring them out in a minute, Joey. How are you? How was the ride over here?"

"Fine, fine, fine," he said. A smile stretched his mouth wide enough to balance his high domed forehead.

A slim young woman in jeans with her long hair tied back was coaxing a slight figure out of the van. "Come on, Brent. This is going to be such fun. Come on out now. Don't be scared." She lifted a kindergarten-sized boy off the steps of the van and set him down. He stood on tiptoe, his hands pressed over his ears as if he feared what he might hear. Then he crept under the van.

"Brent," the woman said. "Don't be like that. Don't you want to see the horses?"

Now an older, heavy set woman in a colorful blouse came down the steps of the van leading a girl who was only a few years younger than Leeann. The girl was dark-haired and pretty, until her face contorted when she tried to say something to the woman.

"A little horse? Yes, I'm sure they can find you a little horse, Barbara," the woman said.

Barbara's foot turned in and down when she walked so that with each step she pulled to one side and seemed about to fall.

Leeann's apprehension about these children increased at the sight of them. How could she be involved in a therapeutic riding program when she didn't understand what these kids' limitations were? It would be difficult enough getting normal children to be comfortable on horseback. These three didn't even have control over their own movements. It was crazy to think they could manage a horse. Where was Mrs. Childs anyway? Leeann was so panicked at the immensity of the task she'd undertaken that she wanted to cut and run. Just then Kristen's mother's car pulled up to the barn next to the van and Kristen, Zach, and Alan got out.

"Here we are, Leeann. What do you want us to do?" Zach asked with a big grin.

She took a deep breath, pretending to be calm. "Hi, guys," she said. "Hanna's in the barn. We're going to lead the horses over to the ring and get the kids acquainted with them, and maybe do some grooming first."

Alan groaned. "Just what I want to do, groom some more horses." He looked doubtfully at the three children who were walking, lurching, or meandering toward the ring with the adults in charge of them. Joey suddenly took off with his arms flapping in the air to meet his mother, who was getting out of her car.

Leeann let out her breath in relief at the sight of Mrs. Childs; she hadn't realized she'd been holding it. Meanwhile, Kristen and Zach were walking toward the barn to get the horses. There was so much to attend to that Leeann barely listened to Mrs. Childs's explanation for being late—something about a board meeting.

"I'm just glad you got here," Leeann said. Then she ran to the barn and led Sassy out first.

"This is it," she told the bright-eyed animal, who kept nudging her arm as he walked on the lead to the ring. "These kids need a lot of help. You better show what a wonderful horse you really are. Okay?" Her chatter was meant more to calm herself than Sassy, who was perfectly at ease since he didn't yet know what was expected of him.

"Why . . . does . . . it do . . . that?" the girl named Barbara anxiously asked the stout woman about the way Sassy kept nudging Leeann.

"This horse is saying, 'Hi, how are you today, good to see you,'" Leeann answered before the woman could say anything. "Sassy's a very friendly horse." Barbara lurched backward, unconvinced, and the woman just managed to catch her before she fell.

Great, Leeann thought to herself. Disaster before we start.

Then Joey, who was holding his mother's hand, noticed Sassy.

"My horse, my horse, my horse!" Joey yelled. He pumped himself up and down as if he were jumping, although his feet never left the ground.

"You want to pet him, Joey? Sassy'd like that. But you have to do it slow and quiet so you don't scare him," Leeann said.

Feeling more confident because of Joey's enthusiasm, she led Sassy through the gate and stopped him next to the mounting block. As soon as Mrs. Childs had guided Joey up onto the block, he launched himself at Sassy's neck and hugged him.

The horse stood calmly.

"I guess Joey's not scared of *his* horse," Leeann said. The mothers laughed politely, and Barbara made a strangled sound.

There were three mounting blocks. Zach approached one, leading a small, light gray horse

141

with a delicate head. "Who'd like to meet Miss Grey?" he asked.

Nobody answered. Joey was brushing Sassy in short chopping motions. "Like this, Joey, like this," Leeann said, trying to guide him into a smoother motion while she kept hold of him so that he wouldn't heave himself off the block in his enthusiasm.

"Where's Joy?" she asked Mrs. Childs.

"Piano lesson," Mrs. Childs said. "She'll come next week. I'm getting her hours changed."

Next time Leeann had a chance to look up, Barbara was on the mounting block next to Miss Grey, being coaxed by both Alan and Zach to touch the animal. "Will . . . she . . . bite me?" Barbara asked timidly.

Brent had to be lifted onto the mounting block by his mother. Kristen was the sidewalker there, and Hanna was holding the lead on fat old Pickles, who had a funny way of wrinkling his lips as if he'd just tasted something sour. Brent wouldn't take the brush, but when Kristen asked him if he wanted to ride the horse, he nodded.

"He's autistic," Mrs. Childs whispered to Leeann. "Doesn't talk, and he's hard to reach although he does understand a lot. Also he's super-sensitive to sounds. I don't envy his mother. Joey's much easier to deal with."

"I wish I knew more about these kids," Leeann said. "I mean, if Kristen and Zach and Alan and I knew more, we'd do a better job."

Mrs. Childs raised an eyebrow. "Good point. We should make educating the trainers about special-needs children a priority. I'll give it some thought." She smiled at Leeann approvingly.

The hour passed swiftly. By the end of it, Joey had ridden Sassy around the ring twice with the help of his sidewalkers and with Hanna leading him. He'd grinned the whole time, so Leeann felt successful with him at least. Still, she was tired by the time the van with their young charges left. To her surprise, she wasn't the only one.

"Whew," Kristen said, "that was a workout. But I think Brent's going to be a good rider. Did you see him smile?"

"Barbara was scared," Alan said. "I couldn't believe how scared that kid was even to go near the horse. But you know what she whispered to me when she left?"

"What?" Zach asked.

"She said, 'Can I have the same horse next time?'"

They all laughed.

"You kids did a great job," Hanna said. "Considering how well things went, Mr. Holden's going to have to give us a next time. And you know who was hanging around the barn watching us?"

"Who?" Leeann asked.

"Amos. I wouldn't be surprised if he joins us one of these days. He's not as hard-hearted as he makes out. More like pig-headed." She laughed.

Leeann gave Sassy a proper grooming and picked his hooves clean before sending him into the corral with the other horses. "Hanna, could we give the horses special treats for being so good with those kids?" she asked.

"Sure. Next time I'll bring a bag of carrots along," Hanna said.

"Don't forget about Saturday," Zach said to Leeann when Kristen's mother arrived to take the volunteers home.

"I won't," Leeann said. "And this time I'll ride Sassy, and I bet Mr. Holden will let you borrow a horse, too, Zach."

"What, you mean you don't want me to ride Paul?" Zach asked in mock dismay.

"Only if you want to," Leeann said.

"No. No, I want to be able to keep up with you. I'll explain it to Paul somehow so as not to hurt his feelings."

"Tell him Sassy sends his regards," Leeann said.

That evening Leeann gave her mother a blow-by-blow account of the first therapeutic riding session, with some input from Hanna, who seemed as exhilarated about it as if she had a stake in the program, too. When the kitchen was cleaned up and Leeann and her mother were crossing the moonlit yard to their cabin, Leeann stopped at the sound of a horse whinnying.

"That sounds like Sassy," she said.

Her mother laughed. "You mean to tell me one horse sounds different from another?"

"Sassy sounds different," Leeann said confidently. She gave a high-pitched whistle in return in case it really had been Sassy.

"I take it now that you can ride, you're happy here?" Rose asked.

"Sure I am. Aren't you, Mama?"

"Well, I'm just wondering what to do about an offer I got." Rose eyed Leeann uneasily.

"An offer?"

"You remember the antique store in Charlotte where I did a lot of business?"

"That old lady with the fluffy purple hair?"

"Lydia. Yes. She wrote me. Said she'd like to make me a partner in her business, no investment necessary, just my charm and hard labor. She's feeling her age and needs help."

"Charlotte," Leeann said thoughtfully. The familiar city she'd grown up in seemed very far away. "What are you going to tell her, Mama?"

"Well, Hanna's not going to need me much longer, you know. I think she can do more right now with the injured hand than she's letting on. And I doubt I want to make a career out of cooking."

"So we're going back?" Unaccountably, Leeann's heart sank.

"I thought maybe you might want to go back," Rose said cautiously. "You left a lot of friends in Charlotte."

"Not really close friends," Leeann said.

"You like the kids here very much, don't you?" Rose said.

"Yes," Leeann admitted. Besides, Zach was here, and Sassy, and the Therapeutic Riding Program.

"Well, we'll think about it," Rose said. "But it is a good offer, Leeann. And I may not get another."

We're going to leave, Leeann thought. *Oh, no, we're going to leave!*

CHAPTER 15 ----------------

When Zach came in late to homeroom the next morning looking glum, Leeann sent him a note asking what was wrong. He passed the note back to her with a scrawl at the bottom that she finally deciphered as, "Can't make it Saturday. Got to help my father do an all-day picnic ride with Peter and Paul. Sorry."

Whenever she glanced at Zach in class, his face was clouded over. Once she even imagined he was about to cry. Surely he couldn't be that disappointed about missing their date. She hoped his mother hadn't gotten worse again.

At lunchtime she stood behind him in the line for pizza and asked, "What's the problem, Zach? Putting off seeing the petroglyphs another week's no big deal, is it?"

He shook his head. "I can't talk about it."

She didn't press him further. Anyway, she had her own inner turmoil. That offer Lydia had made to Rose. Having to leave Lost River Ranch just when life was coming together for her here would be rotten luck. Now she not only had friends, she had Sassy to ride. Even when she'd dreamed of owning her own horse, Leeann had never imagined one with as much personality as Sassy. He seemed almost human, a companion to share experiences with. And how could she betray the warm welcome of her new friends by telling them that she was leaving them when she had barely arrived?

After school, Leeann rode Sassy over to Joy's house. While she was tying him to the rail, Joey came running down to the ring. "Up, up, up," he yelled, flapping his arms

"Hold it a second. Ho, Joey," she said and let him hug her.

Joy came out of her house, followed by her mother. "Can you help me get Joey up on Sassy?" Leeann asked them.

"Oh, you don't have to do that," Mrs. Childs said.

"But I want to," Leeann said.

"I'll saddle Dancer so I can ride with you," Joy said. She ran off to the barn.

While Joey was climbing the mounting block, holding his mother's hand, Leeann shortened the stirrups as far as they would go. Then she patiently taught Joey all over again how to grip some of the horse's mane and put his foot into the stirrup. Even so, it took both her and Enid Childs to heave him into the saddle.

"There you go," Leeann said. "Now can you sit

very still by yourself, and I'll lead Sassy around the ring?"

Joey wriggled in excitement. "Look at me, Joyee," he squealed at his sister, who was settling the saddle onto Dancer. Joy nodded at him, busy with her own mount. Joey let go of the horn to wave his hands about.

"Joey," his mother protested, "you have to hold on or you'll fall off. I'll be his sidewalker," she said to Leeann. "Do you think it's safe with just the two of us?"

"Well, he should have a helmet," Leeann said.

"Oh, right." Mrs. Childs made Joy dismount and go to the barn to get one. Leeann wondered why Joy couldn't be the second sidewalker and do her own riding after Joey was finished. But since neither Joy nor her mother seemed to think of that, she decided it wasn't her business to suggest it.

"Can you sit straight in the saddle so you won't slide off, Joey?" Leeann asked as Joey leaned sideways to look ahead of Sassy.

Joey tried, but his cheeks were flushed with excitement and his wide-set eyes were wild. Sassy patiently stood still as if he understood the instability of his rider. When Joy had delivered the helmet and her brother had it on, Leeann led Sassy around the ring. Joey chortled and squealed. His mother had to struggle to keep him upright in the saddle.

"Again?" Leeann asked Joey when they'd returned to where they'd started.

"Leeann," Joy protested. "He had his ride. Come on. Ride with me."

"Again. Again," Joey said.

"One more time," Mrs. Childs said. "You'll get your turn, Joy."

Leeann blocked out Joy's complaints and busied herself reminding Joey how to hold the reins. "Don't pull on them or you'll hurt Sassy's mouth," she said.

Immediately, Joey clutched the reins to his chest, looking scared. "I hurt horsey?" he asked after they'd circled the ring again.

"No, you were a good boy, Joey."

"Come on, Leeann. Let's go," Joy called impatiently. She was waiting at the corral gate.

Suddenly Joey's face changed and he looked ready to cry. "Down," he said. "Down, down, down."

He slumped off the horse, not listening to Leeann, who was trying to teach him how to dismount onto the block. "He didn't sleep a lot last night. And anyway he gets tired really fast," Mrs. Childs explained. She caught him as he tumbled onto the mounting block. "Thanks, Leeann," she said. "You gave him a real treat."

She took Joey into the house. Leeann adjusted the stirrups back to suit herself and mounted Sassy. "Okay, I'm ready," she told Joy.

They walked their horses to the edge of a dry river wash, the rocky banks of which were studded with bushes and occasional palo verde trees, green even to their trunks and branches. Joy said when the seasonal rains filled it, the river ran through the middle of the Childses' forty-acre property.

"We can run the horses full out here," she said. "How about it?"

Leeann grinned. "Sounds good to me." They sat back in their saddles and let the horses pick their way down the steep bank to the flat wash, which made a wide road of pale sand. "I'll race you to those big white tree trunks down there." Leeann pointed toward a bend in the river a quarter of a mile away.

"The sycamores? Fine. Let's go!" Joy said. She kicked Dancer and screamed when the horse reared up, but she kept her seat and Dancer took off at a wild gallop.

It was the stuff of Leeann's dreams She leaned forward in the saddle and loosened the reins some. Without any further encouragement, Sassy took off after Dancer at a controlled canter that felt smooth as riding a magic carpet. What a horse Sassy was! Leeann's grin nearly jumped off her face. She'd never been happier.

"Whoa, ho up, ho," Joy was yelling at Dancer as she tugged on the reins to slow him. Dancer tossed his head as if he wanted to rip the reins from Joy's hands. When Sassy drew alongside him, Leeann pulled Sassy back into a trot and Dancer slowed to keep pace. The two animals stepped along smartly side by side.

"Boy, did he scare me!" Joy said. "I thought he was going to run away with me. It's a good thing you were here, Leeann."

The two horses were bumping against each other companionably now and walking along like old friends.

"This is so wonderful. This is the best," Leeann exulted.

"Even though it's just you and me and Zach's not here?" Joy teased.

"It couldn't be better," Leeann said.

"But you like Zach a lot, don't you?" Joy asked.

"Sure. He's a nice kid."

"I'm glad. You know, he used to like Kristen, but she never liked him back. So it's just Alan and me and it feels kind of weird being the only couple in our class. It's nice that there'll be you and Zach, too."

"Joy," Leeann said, "don't plan on anything."

"Why not? You said you like him and he's obviously crazy about you."

Leeann sighed. As they turned the horses around and headed them back, she told Joy about her mother's job offer.

"Tell her not to take it," Joy urged. "Leeann, you tell her you'll die if you leave here now. You can't go. What would happen to the Therapeutic Riding Program?"

"Your mother will keep it going just fine without me. Don't worry."

"But Joey would miss you, and so would I. Maybe you don't believe me because you haven't been here that long, but you fit. You really fit here, Leeann. You know what I mean?"

Tears stung Leeann's eyes. "Yes, I know," she said. Joy had said it just right. She fit. She fit perfectly in this place.

"Did you tell Zach?" Joy asked.

Sassy stumbled and Leeann pulled up on her reins. "No. And don't you. Don't tell anyone, Joy. I'm not sure we're going yet anyway."

"But you think your mother wants to go?"

"Probably."

"That rots. Poor Zach. Poor everybody. That really rots." They had come to soft ground, and Joy led them up a gully in the riverbank onto the cactus-studded desert.

"Zach's really a lot nicer than Alan," Joy mused after she'd wearied of lamenting the possibility of Leeann's leaving. "You know what Alan did to me?"

"No, what?" Leeann was relieved to stop talking about herself and settle into listening, which was the role she was most comfortable playing in her relationships with other kids. Joy unwound an endless story about how Alan had invited her to his house and then forgotten she was coming and gone somewhere else. "I was so embarrassed. I had to tell his mother he'd asked me to come, and then I had to go back to the car and tell my mother he wasn't there. He's really going to have to crawl to make me forgive him for this one," Joy said.

I like her, Leeann thought in the midst of her listening daze. True, Joy was a little spoiled and self-centered, but she was lively and goodhearted. Were there any friends left in Charlotte she had liked better? No, Leeann realized. Not one.

Dancer spooked as a roadrunner dashed in front of him. The tall, stiff bird disappeared behind a thorny bush, but Dancer had reared up and Joy was nearly unseated. "Down, boy," she ordered shrilly. "Down, Dancer."

The palomino took off at a canter back toward the river. Leeann turned Sassy and kicked him into a gallop that cut across Joy's path so as to keep her and her horse from getting hurt crashing down the riverbank. Sassy snorted and stopped sideways to the edge. Dancer braked to a stop just short of banging into him.

"Whew!" Joy said when she'd resettled herself on the saddle. "That was scary. You saved my neck, Leeann."

"Sassy did. He did that like a cow pony, didn't he?"

"Yeah, you've got a smart horse there."

"Sassy's not my horse," Leeann said soberly.

"I know. I mean . . ." Joy sounded embarrassed. "Oh, Leeann, you can't leave us."

Leeann bent over Sassy's neck and buried her face in the coarse black mane. She wasn't one to cry, but she felt close to tears now. How could everything so right be so close to going wrong?

That night in bed Leeann looked out at the sliver of lemon moon and tried thinking about how it had been in Charlotte. She flashed on a memory of a sleepover with the two good friends who'd moved away. They'd practiced kissing and told each other their secrets and stayed awake so long they'd watched the dawn come up. If it could only be like that again, she wouldn't mind so much having her mother take that partnership Lydia had offered. After all, she'd spent some really happy years in Charlotte. Only now her happiness lay here.

The horse project group worked hard in class Monday. Each had written between five and ten pages on his or her subject. That is, except for Alan, who had filled up his pages with a few very brief paragraphs about his sisters' horses and a lot of clever pen sketches of his sisters on their mounts. Leeann had had so much to say about Sassy's escapades that she'd had to cut some of it to keep to the ten-page maximum Ms. Morabita had decided to impose.

Joy asked if Leeann would bring her camera over that afternoon to take pictures of her riding Dancer to use for the project report. She invited Kristen, too.

"I can't come," Kristen said. "I have to go visit

155

sick people in the nursing home with my mother and grandmother." She wrinkled her nose as if she wasn't looking forward to it.

That afternoon, Joey was much more relaxed when Leeann put him on Sassy for a brief ride. It was his third riding experience.

Mrs. Childs said to Leeann, "You know, at Joey's school, there's so much interest in our therapeutic riding sessions that I had to put people on a waiting list. Too bad we can't get Amos and his wranglers to help us so we could have a bigger group."

"Maybe if you talk to Mr. Holden, Amos could be persuaded." Leeann remembered that Amos had given her good advice about putting Sassy in the barn, although lately Sassy had been around anyway when he was needed. Still, the advice had been positive, the first positive thing Amos had ever said to her.

The therapeutic riding session went well that Thursday. Brent wouldn't brush his horse, but he took the reins and turned the horse left and right as his sidewalkers suggested. "You're a regular jockey," Kristen told him. "Now what you have to do is tell the horse when you want to stop, Brent. You can say, 'ho,' can't you? It's such a little word. Just 'ho.' Say it, Brent. Come on, say it for me."

Joey was yelling "ho" every other minute. Sassy would come to a halt and Joey would laugh as if it tickled him to have the big animal obey him.

Alan actually coaxed Barbara onto the gray

horse this session, although she somehow ended up sitting backward in the saddle and Alan and Zach had a hard time getting her turned around one leg at a time. It was funny to watch the two boys encouraging Barbara to move. All three of them were so awkward and earnest at the same time.

Zach had been subdued all week. Leeann kept waiting for him to tell her what was wrong, but he didn't. He did ask her if they could try to go see the petroglyphs next Saturday and she had agreed. Maybe when they were alone he would share his problem, whatever it was. She might be ready to share her news with him by then as well.

On Friday Zach told the lunch group that he had a great idea. "Why don't we put on a rodeo with the kids?"

"A rodeo?" Joy said. "Zach, they're not exactly expert riders yet."

"A rodeo that fits what they can do," Zach persisted.

"Like?" Leeann asked.

"Oh, like that exercise Joy's mother was telling us about where they pick up a ring and carry it on horseback to someplace else and put it down. That could be one event. And leading the horse around a barrel could be another."

"And just sitting right in the saddle all the way around the ring, that could get them points," Kristen said with immediate enthusiasm.

"And everybody wins," Leeann said. She nodded. "That *is* a great idea, Zach. Let's do it."

Mrs. Childs said the parents on her waiting list would want to attend the rodeo, and all the interest might help persuade Mr. Holden to go into the program in a bigger way. The rodeo was set for the last Thursday of the month.

Friday evening Leeann was eagerly telling her mother how she expected Joey to shine when Rose said, "I guess we could wait until after the rodeo to leave."

"To leave?" Leeann went into shock.

"Honey?" Rose looked startled. "You knew we were going, didn't you?"

"No. How would I know? You didn't say anything. I thought you were still thinking about it."

"But Leeann." Rose bit her lip. "You realize I don't have any choice. *We* don't have any choice. I've got to make a living for us, and I can't depend on making it here. You knew that, honey. Didn't you?"

"But couldn't you wait a while? I mean, at least until they shut down Lost River Ranch for the summer. Then school would be over and I wouldn't have to change in the middle again. Couldn't we stay just until then?"

"The thing is, Lydia can't handle things back in Charlotte by herself much longer, and Hanna's healed so fast. She doesn't need me, and it's not fair for Mr. Holden to pay for two cooks when he can only afford one."

"Oh, Mama," Leeann sighed. "Oh, Mama." She felt as grieved as she had when Big John had left them, as grieved as when her best friends had both moved away from Charlotte in the same year. Why couldn't things work out well for her, just once?

CHAPTER 16 ————————

Saturday Leeann awoke to a cloudless sky so blue it hurt her eyes. It was winter back East, but even in the cool of morning she didn't need a jacket here. The day couldn't have been more perfect for the picnic ride to see the petroglyphs. She wasn't as eager for it as she might have been, though, weighed down as she was with bad news. She couldn't decide whether to unload it on Zach immediately and risk ruining the day, or not tell him she was leaving Arizona and maybe make him angry at her for deceiving him.

Everything started out well. Rose packed four different kinds of leftover meat and vegetable salads for her. Zach arrived on Paul and turned the Percheron loose in the corral. He trotted the lively bay mare Amos had saddled for him around the corral to see how she behaved and thanked Amos enthusiastically for her. Meanwhile, Leeann secured their picnic lunch bag and a gallon of water to Sassy's saddle and mounted him.

"Don't lather the horses up too hard," Amos

said. "Take it slow and easy. It's gonna be hot later." He checked Sassy's cinch belt and nodded approvingly. Leeann even thought he might be about to smile at her, but he didn't quite.

"Thanks, Amos. I hope you have a good day," she told him.

"I got to go to town," he said. "Got to see a dentist."

"Oh, well, I hope he fixes you up fast then," she said.

"Only way to fix the holes I got is to pull the teeth."

Leeann swallowed and said cautiously. "I hope he doesn't do that."

"Don't matter. I'd just as well be rid of them. What's gone can't ache."

Leeann gulped and gave up trying to encourage him. She just waved goodbye, and she and Zach set off side by side toward the mountains.

The landscape that had seemed to take so long to cover on Paul rolled past them with ease now that they were riding Sassy and the frisky bay. The horses moved at a brisk pace, as if taking a trip on a morning like this was their own idea of a fun time. Sassy's ears turned forward to hear the wind through the tall grasses near the riverbed and back to hear Leeann's murmurs of encouragement. He dipped his head sideways at the family of Gambel's quail that rushed across their path in line with each other like windup toys, the single feather at the top of each head aquiver. His nostrils flared at the sweet scent of some desert plant that Leeann couldn't identify. "Happy?" Leeann asked him. "Of course you are."

The question was, how was Zach doing? He was so quiet, and Leeann didn't know him well enough to guess if that meant something was wrong or if he was just enjoying the peace of the morning. They splashed through a shallow but fast-running stream and climbed a rocky bank to the desert, where they rode past one sculptured hill after another. Zach would talk when he was ready, Leeann thought, and like Sassy she concentrated on opening her senses to the magic of the ride.

They got to the canyon so quickly that it wasn't quite eleven when they secured the horses to a boulder near the basin of water where Sassy had gotten his hoof caught. "Should we eat lunch now?" Leeann asked.

"Fine with me," Zach said. "I can always eat."

They found a rock flat as a tabletop, where Leeann laid the food out, and then they set to. Today Zach barely commented on the lunch. He seemed so lost in himself that Leeann wondered if he even knew what he was eating. When they'd finished, he helped her pack their leftovers into the picnic bag. Leeann fed Sassy the apple she'd saved for him. Sassy relished it with a happy chomping that showed more pleasure in the treat than Zach had displayed at his whole feast.

They left the horses and climbed up the spill of boulders to the ledge where the petroglyphs were painted in red and black on the wall of a natural cave. It was open along its length on the canyon side and ran fifty feet or so before it diminished to nothing. It was shaded from the sun most of the day, but even in the dim light Leeann was amazed to see dozens of running deer chased by a few solitary stick figures that obviously represented the hunters.

"It's wonderful," Leeann said. She was awestruck by this vision of human beings who might have been living when Columbus set sail on his voyage of discovery, or even before, at a time when the United States belonged solely to the Native Americans who inhabited it.

"See the antlers on this one?" Zach said. "And the way this deer's looking back over its shoulder? I couldn't draw them that well on paper, and he carved it on a rock wall."

"Or she," Leeann said.

"Yeah, but it was probably a he. Males were the hunters. The women stayed home and made baskets and grew corn and stuff like that."

"You think women can't do art as well as men?"

"I didn't say that. I just said mostly males did the hunting," Zach said. "Listen, I admire the females in my life more than the males. Except for my dad. Are you an artist, Leeann?"

"No, not really. The only kind of art I'm any

good at is photography, and I'm just a beginner at that." They studied the wall a while longer, taking note of the twisting heads and kicked-up rear hooves of the deer, and the spear poised to be thrown above a stick figure's shoulder.

Leeann had brought her camera. She took a whole roll of pictures, telling herself that she'd probably never see this spot again. Still Zach hadn't confided what was bothering him, and she hadn't told him that she was leaving.

There was a moment when she stepped back to get a better angle and bumped into Zach, who grabbed her arm to steady her. He might have pulled her to him and kissed her then, but he didn't.

Finally, she asked, "What's bothering you, Zach?"

"I don't want to mess up our day by talking about it," he said. His face was as shadowed as the mountains under clouds.

"It's no good," she said. "You have to tell me what's been eating you. I've watched you being miserable for more than a week now."

"You could tell, huh?"

"Yeah." She nodded.

He hunkered down on his heels and stared out into the canyon. "I'll say one thing, Leeann," he said huskily. "You're the only good thing happening to me. And this place . . ." He looked around the cave. "Well, I guess it's just a curiosity to you, but it's sort of sacred to me, and being here with you means a lot to me. I mean, I'm going to remember it my whole life."

His solemn tone touched her. She sat down on the ground beside him.

"But I shouldn't have come," he continued.

"Why not?"

"My mother couldn't talk this morning. I mean, she couldn't say anything. Her voicebox just . . . I really shouldn't have left her." He shook his head as if in disgust at himself. "But I came anyway."

"I'm sorry, Zach."

"Yeah, I'm a rotten egg."

"No, you're not," Leeann said. "I bet she wanted you to come. I bet she did, didn't she?"

He shrugged. "Maybe."

Down in the canyon below them, Sassy was teasing Zach's bay, ducking his head and pretending to nip at the bay's leg. The bay fended him off with a backward flip of her head, baring her teeth at Sassy's neck. Sassy moved around and tried for the bay's back leg. The bay kicked up her heels at Sassy, but gently as if she understood it was all in play.

"It must be horrible," Leeann said, "I mean, to see your mother that way."

"Yeah, I love her a lot," Zach said. "She's always treated me like I was a prize. She can make me feel good just by the way she looks at me." He sighed. "I'm sorry. I shouldn't have said anything. Now I've ruined the day for you."

"No, you haven't. Not yet anyway. And if you'll just hold still a minute more, my day will be perfect," she said.

He frowned in puzzlement at her. But she took his long face in her two hands and kissed him briefly on the lips. "I like you a lot, Zach," she said. "And I don't think you should feel guilty about your mother. Everybody needs time off, and you certainly deserve it."

Without waiting for him to react, she started down the slide of rocks toward the canyon floor and Sassy. Zach followed. She wouldn't tell him she was leaving, she decided. Not today. Not when he was dealing with so much misery already.

They led the horses through the narrow keyhole out of the canyon, mounted them, and started back. Zach's horse allowed Sassy to lead the way, and Sassy kept breaking into a trot whenever Leeann gave him half an excuse. Every time he did it on his own, he'd tip his ears back as if to hear if Leeann was going to scold him. Once he ducked his head and lightly grabbed Leeann's toe boot in his big teeth.

"Stop that." Leeann swatted Sassy away from her foot. It seemed that Sassy was the one most fully enjoying the ride. Not having much sense of the future had its advantages, Leeann thought.

"See you in school Monday," Zach said after he'd switched from the bay to Paul and was ready to set off for home. "Thanks, Leeann. Thanks for . . . you know." He blushed.

166

Yes, it was good she hadn't told him. At least she'd left him happy about something, even if it was only a kiss from a girl who wasn't going to be around to comfort him for long.

"And you, Sassy, will you miss me, too?" Leeann asked the horse as she wiped him down and began to brush his dusty coat. Not as much as she'd miss him, Leeann thought. Sassy might not be hers, but he was as close as she was ever likely to get to having a horse of her own.

CHAPTER 17 ——————————

It had become a ritual with Leeann to walk out to the corral with a treat for Sassy after she finished her homework at night. Now that it was March, the night air had become silky cool instead of cold. The sky made a spangled canopy over the horses, who shifted about and sighed as they dozed. Sometimes she'd hear the coyotes' eerie howling. Sometimes dark wings sailed past her head. But Sassy always came to the fence and nuzzled Leeann affectionately as he took his treat, and this was always a blissful moment.

Then came the night Rose stopped her as she was about to leave the cabin for the corral. "Leeann, hold up a while. We've got to talk." Rose tossed her magazine onto the floor and uncurled her legs.

"Not now, Rose."

"Now," Rose said. "That horse of yours can wait."

"Sassy's not my horse."

"Around here they talk as if he is. Hanna says you've got him so tamed he doesn't run away anymore. Apparently even Amos is impressed."

"Sassy's one reason why I don't want to talk about leaving," Leeann said soberly.

"It's not like you to hide your head in the sand."

Leeann perched on the edge of the couch thumbing the carrot, staring at its knobby length instead of at her mother's face. "Hiding's all I can do, because you're the one directing our lives. I just have to go along."

"Leeann, don't make me out to be a tyrant. I know you like it here. And you know if I had any alternative to accepting Lydia's offer, we'd stay."

Leeann drew a deep breath and spaced the words out carefully as she said, "I really don't want to go back to Charlotte, Rose."

"But honey, Lydia's offer is the best I'm likely to get. And it isn't as if Charlotte was such a bad place for you, was it?"

"But I'm happier here." Leeann was thinking of Kristen and Zach. "I mean, it's not just Sassy. People need me here."

"Well, what do you want me to do? Take any kind of work so we can stay? There's a job as a gas station attendant I could try for, but I'm pretty old to be pumping gas. Besides, we couldn't live on what it would pay."

"Mr. Holden couldn't keep two cooks?"

"You know he can't. And Hanna's already lifting heavy pots when she thinks I don't see her . . . I'm thinking we should leave the end of this month."

Leeann caught her breath. Having a set time

169

for their departure was what she had been avoiding.

"The longer you stay, the harder it will be to go," Rose said.

Leeann shook her head. She couldn't imagine loving Sassy more or being any more deeply involved with the Therapeutic Riding Program and her friends than she already was.

"I don't know what to say, love," Rose said. "You know I'd do a lot to make you happy. "

"I know," Leeann said.

When Big John had left them, Rose had refused to sit around feeling sorry for herself. She'd straightened her back and said, "My daddy always told me a disappointment is just a challenge in disguise." Then she had set about rebuilding their lives. Leeann had admired her mother for that. Now it was her turn to refuse to feel sorry for herself.

"Well, I guess I'll go tell Sassy the bad news," she said. And because her mother's amber eyes were so sad, she added, "It's okay, Mama. I'll get over it."

"There's my girl," Rose said with obvious relief.

Leeann left the cabin wishing she didn't understand, wishing she could rage and scream and demand Rose stay here. That would have been a lot easier than trying to be sensible.

Her boots crunched on the dried mud near the corral. Tonight Sassy was waiting for her at the fence without needing to be called. He took his carrot and she threaded her fingers through the long coarse hairs of his mane, smoothing it to one side. "I'm going to miss you," she said.

Sassy munched companionably, then pushed his moleskin-soft muzzle at her hand. "That's it," Leeann said. "I don't have any more." But Sassy kept nudging. "You're just being affectionate, aren't you? You're such a love, Sassy." She leaned her cheek against the horse's neck and breathed deep of the comfortable smell of dew and warm animal. "I wish I'd been born out here. I wish I could stay on this ranch with you forever."

At lunch the next day Leeann told her group that she was leaving and when. Zach looked as if she'd hit him.

Joy said, "Oh, no, Leeann. That's awful!"

And Kristen chimed in with, "But what about the Therapeutic Riding Program?"

"You'll have to get someone else to help out with it," Leeann said.

"It's not fair. You can't go," Kristen said.

Alan wanted to know where she was going and when she told him, he said, "Charlotte, North Carolina? You won't even be able to afford a plane ticket to come back if you're going that far away."

"Maybe I can do some babysitting and save up and visit you guys next summer." Leeann looked at Zach. He wouldn't meet her eyes.

Joy said, "You could come for the whole summer and stay with me. I've got twin beds in my bedroom and my own bathroom. My folks like you a lot, Leeann. Besides, Joey would be thrilled if you stayed with us."

"You think your mother would let you do that, Leeann?" Kristen asked.

"She might," Leeann said hopefully.

"I could hold a bake sale to make money toward your plane ticket," Kristen said.

"Oh, Kristen, you're too much." Leeann hugged her. Then she said, "But let's not talk about this anymore, okay?" She was afraid she'd start crying if they did.

Zach was chewing on his lip and glowering at the toe end of his boot as if he'd had all he could take of the subject as well. It was a relief when the conversation turned to more immediate worries, like the social studies test that afternoon. The end of lunch came and they set off for class together, but Zach still hadn't said a word.

The therapeutic riding session hit a few bumps that Thursday. First of all, Barbara didn't show. Then Kristen's favorite child, the autistic boy Brent, leaned so far over to hug his horse's short, stout neck that his slight body slid around under it. The horse stopped in its tracks while Brent clung to its neck screeching until Kristen was able to release his grasp on it. Next he transferred his stranglehold to her. "You're choking me, Brent," she gasped.

Leeann left Joey on the mounting block and rushed over to unclench Brent from Kristen.

While Leeann's back was turned, Joey mounted Sassy from the block by himself—backwards. He insisted on sitting the horse backward once around the ring while he beamed proudly.

Zach was out of school the next Monday, and no one answered the phone at his house when Leeann called to find out how he was. Tuesday he returned to school, and when they happened to meet at their lockers, Zach told Leeann that his mother had been hospitalized. She'd had a cold that wouldn't go away. It had started the day he and Leeann had gone to see the petroglyphs. "I shouldn't have left her that day," he said. "I knew she was sick but I went anyway. I wish I hadn't left her."

"How's she doing now?" Leeann asked.

He shrugged. "She's having trouble breathing."

"But she's not going to die, Zach. Is she?"

"I don't know. Last summer she promised me she wouldn't until I'm out of high school. But no one can promise something like that. I don't know what Pop'd do if we lost her." Zach looked at Leeann with so much anguish, she could only squeeze his hand and then hug him hard.

"If you lose your mother," she advised him finally, "your father'll feel terrible. And then he'll recover. My mother did. People just do, even if it seems they can't."

Zach sighed deeply. "Could be he'll sell everything and go to Alaska or something like that. He talks about living on a river someday, where it's still wild country, and his kind of skills would make him a living. If he did that and he wanted me to go with him, I'd go maybe for a while. But I don't want to live where there's no people. I want to get trained for a job, like with computers or something, that would keep me in some half-civilized place." He smiled. "Like here."

"You're smart enough to go to college, Zach."

"No chance of that. Pop's got no money and I'm not likely to win any athletic scholarships. Maybe I'll join the service and get Uncle Sam to train me for something."

"You sure think far ahead."

He nodded and said gruffly. "The other thing I'm afraid he might do is off himself after my mother's gone."

"Kill himself?"

"Yeah."

"He wouldn't do that to you."

"Yeah, he might. He keeps telling me how tough I am, how I can do everything for myself. I think he's getting ready to leave me one way or the other."

"Zach, she's still alive, and she may be for years and years. And if she dies, you don't know what he'll do."

He smiled at her. "You know," he said, "I'd be

174

pretty depressed if I didn't have you to talk to."

And she was leaving. They both knew she was leaving in less than two weeks, and they had both chosen to pretend it wasn't so.

CHAPTER 18 ––––––––––––––

The rodeo for the special-needs kids was to take place on the last Thursday of the month, just before Leeann had to leave for Charlotte. Her friends were so involved in planning for the rodeo that it was all they talked about when they were together, as if her leaving weren't going to happen, or as if it didn't matter.

Zach was in charge of events. Kristen was doing signs and publicity. Joy was seeing to refreshments. Leeann had the responsibility for the horses and equipment, and she was the liaison with the people at the ranch. That meant she had to speak to Amos, which turned out to be easy. Now that she was leaving, Amos seemed to have accepted her. He even promised to have the three horses she needed back early so that she'd have time to groom them. And he agreed that it was all right if her friends helped her with the grooming, since there'd be less than an hour to get the horses ready.

"I'll be around if you need me during the rodeo," he offered.

Leeann thanked him. And when she noticed that he was moving stiffly, as if his arthritis had its claws in him, she made herself useful by taking the tack from the horses he was unsaddling and hanging it back up in the barn for him.

Mr. Holden had agreed to preside as ringmaster for the rodeo, so long as he could invite his guests to come down to the corral and watch if they wanted to. When Mrs. Childs and the other parents got involved, the adults uncovered a dozen new details that needed pinning down. The logistics became so complex that Leeann was glad nobody had realized beforehand what was necessary. They might never have undertaken the project.

In the excitement of rodeo day, even Leeann stopped thinking about having to leave that weekend. Attracted by the colorful signs and strings of balloons and streamers, guests from the ranch lined the ring. A stiff breeze made the sun's heat pleasurable.

Several families Leeann didn't know arrived with their special-needs children. From the quick course of training Mrs. Childs had given the volunteers, Leeann could identify two wheelchair-bound girls as having cerebral palsy. Mrs. Childs had said the next step in the program was to include wheelchair-bound kids. Leeann was sorry she wouldn't be around to see how that would go.

The three rodeo contestants arrived in costume. Joey was dressed as a jockey in red and green riding silks. Little Brent was Superman, with a red cape, blue tights and shirt, and a red *S* on his narrow chest. Barbara was a princess, a pretty one, if a little awkward in her movements. All three children wore their regulation hard-topped riding hats.

Alan and Zach had on cowboy hats and boots and wore the red bandannas Mrs. Childs had purchased to identify the volunteers. Leeann was wearing a straw hat since she didn't own a cowboy hat. Joy looked like a Barbie doll in her white stetson and a white western shirt. But Kristen had a red and white bicycle helmet to go with her red bandanna.

"I wanted the kids to see me wearing safe headgear for riding even if it looks weird," Kristen said.

"You don't look weird and you're right," Leeann told her. "I'll go borrow Hanna's motorcycle helmet."

"No, don't leave now." Kristen grabbed her arm. "It looks like Mr. Holden's starting us off on time. I hope nothing goes wrong. I hope our kids don't fall off or cry. I didn't sleep last night thinking about all the things that could go wrong."

Leeann laughed. "It's going to be great," she said.

At that moment Zach appeared beside her. Something sad about his eyes made Leeann ask, "How's your mother doing now that she's out of the hospital?"

"Not too bad. She smiled at me this morning."

"Good," Leeann said. She hoped his mother had lots of smiles left in her for Zach.

Mr. Holden had climbed on top of a picnic table in the center of the ring. He spoke through a bullhorn as he explained what a therapeutic riding program was. He said he was proud that Lost River Ranch was involved in this very special rodeo, first of its kind in the area, maybe the first of its kind anywhere for all they knew. He asked the audience to begin by giving the contestants—none of whom had been on a horse until a couple of months ago—a big hand. The audience clapped and whistled enthusiastically.

"All rodeo riders are required to walk their mounts around the ring and return to starting position," Mr. Holden said, and then sounding like a real ringmaster, he announced, "And here comes our first rider, happy cowboy Joey Childs, riding Sassy."

Joey, as the most experienced rider among the special-needs kids, rode in on Sassy without a leader. Joy and Leeann were his sidewalkers. He waved grandly at the audience with one hand and held onto his saddle horn with the other. "Hi, hi, hi!" he yelled happily.

"Hi," the audience chorused back, as ebullient as the balloons and flags tossing in the breeze over their heads.

Into the ring following Joey came Brent, who

had flopped backward in the saddle so he was lying along the horse's back. Kristen was talking at him determinedly as she walked alongside him. His mother was on the other side of him, and Hanna was leading the horse.

"Sit up, Brent. Can't you sit up? You're on parade," Kristen begged in dismay. But the audience, thinking Brent was doing some kind of trick, cheered and clapped for him warmly.

Barbara came next. She sat beautifully straight-backed, gripping the saddle horn and smiling proudly with Zach and Alan on either side of her like courtiers, and her mother leading the horse.

"Nice job, princess," someone in the audience yelled and someone else whistled. Barbara laughed out loud.

The next event was the rings. Each rider had to approach Leeann, who held a ring up where it could be reached easily. When Barbara's hand didn't connect with the ring, Leeann slipped it onto her wrist. Then each rider had to direct his or her horse to the other side of the corral, where Mr. Holden received the rings and thanked each child.

Brent sat up on his horse this time, but he wouldn't let go of his ring no matter how Kristen tried to persuade him to. Mr. Holden finally had to let him keep it. Kristen looked as if she might burst into tears.

Joey, with just Joy as his sidewalker and no leader, managed to walk Sassy around a barrel and under a string of balloons for the next event.

He was supposed to be the only contestant, but Barbara wanted to go too, so she was allowed to try it. She walked her horse twice around the barrel and nearly fell off when she suddenly reached up to grab at a balloon. Zach caught her just in time as the audience cried out in alarm.

Carrots figured in the next event. Each child had to dismount onto the mounting block with as little assistance as possible, take a carrot from Leeann, feed it to his horse, then pat the horse and thank it for the good job it had done.

Brent, who had never uttered anything but unintelligble cries as far as Leeann knew, drew himself up straight in the saddle at the mounting block and said, "Ho." Loud and clear.

His horse stopped instantly and Kristen yelled, "Brent, you talked!"

Her excitement alerted the audience to the uniqueness of the happening, and they whistled and clapped. Kristen grabbed Brent when he got off Sassy and hugged him. He pulled away. But then he turned back, and Leeann saw him sign something to Kristen.

"What did he say?" Leeann asked after she'd given Brent his carrot and he'd properly fed his horse.

Kristen was so moved that she had tears in her eyes and could hardly speak. "He said 'I love you,'" she choked out. "It's the only sign I've learned so far."

For the last exercise Zach had labeled one of the big trash barrels "The Wishing Well" and decorated it in bright red crepe paper. He set the barrel in the arena, and Mr. Holden explained through his bullhorn that each child was to whisper a wish to Zach, who'd write it on a slip of paper. Then the child was to lead his horse to the barrel and drop the slip of paper into it.

Barbara whispered something when she had lurched beside her patient pinto to the barrel. "Sure, your wish could come true," Zach told her.

Music had been provided for the final ride out of the arena. As "Happy Trails to You" sounded on the tape deck, each child mounted his horse again and rode it once around the arena and out through the gate.

"Bye, bye, bye," Joey shouted.

Brent went around with his head buried in his horse's mane this time. Nonetheless, the audience called goodbye to him, and Kristen waved shyly at them in his stead.

Barbara was tired. She didn't want to remount her horse. She clung to Alan, so he got on her horse and Zach lifted her up in front of Alan. Alan held the exhausted child in his arms while she waved goodbye at her appreciative audience.

"Bye princess," someone called out. "Bye, bye, bye."

"The rodeo was a smash hit," Enid Childs said to Leeann and Zach as they stood holding the gate to the ring open. "You'll never know how much it did for these kids! It was wonderful. You were wonderful. Thanks." She gave them each a kiss on a cheek.

"Nice lady," Zach said when Mrs. Childs had gone off to where her car was parked. He held out a piece of paper still remaining from the sheet he'd torn up. "One wish left for you, Leeann. What's it to be?"

"Oh, I don't know," she said distractedly. She was watching the people straggling off to their cars, or back to the ranch house, with relief that it was over and satisfaction that it had been a success.

"Well, I know what you wish," he said, and he scribbled something on the paper. "Here, go put it in the wishing well."

She took the folded sheet with a smile and peeked inside it before dropping it into the barrel. "I wish for a horse of my own," he had written for her.

"Did I get it right?" he asked when she returned to him.

She shook her head. "No. Believe it or not, I haven't been thinking about that for a while."

"So what's your wish, then?" he asked.

"That we could all stay as happy as we were this afternoon. The rodeo was a great idea, Zach." She smiled at him.

And that was when he kissed her, soft and sweet.

CHAPTER 19 ----------------

Leeann came out of the kiss and saw Amos storming toward her.

"What's wrong?" she asked anxiously as he planted himself squarely in front of her.

"That woman wants them out of wheelchairs and on horseback next. She's crazy, and I won't have nothing to do with it. Nothing. No way."

"The parents will take responsibility, Amos," Leeann spoke quietly to calm him. He was so agitated he was shaking.

"No. I can't deal with that woman. You want to stay here and deal with her, then maybe. But I'm not having any truck with her on my own." He made an about-face and marched off.

Zach was red in the face with suppressed laughter. As soon as Amos was safely in the barn, the sound burst from Zach like a firecracker on the Fourth of July.

"What's so funny?" Leeann asked.

Zach got control of himself finally and answered, "Amos needs you, Leeann. Did you hear him? I can't believe it. What'd you do to him?"

"Nothing," she said. "I guess he just realized that I'm dependable."

"Yeah." Zach was grinning at her with admiration. Then he grew thoughtful. "You know something," he said. "If you're game to stay here a little longer, we might be able to use old Amos as a lever."

"I'd love to stay longer," she said. But she had no idea what Zach was getting at.

Instead of explaining, he turned and ran over to the parking area where Mrs. Childs had lingered to chat with some of the parents of the special-needs children who had come to watch the rodeo. Joy and Alan were chasing Joey around the ramada, empty now because the ranch guests had gone to change for dinner.

Kristen was talking to her mother, who'd just arrived. Nobody had unsaddled the three horses that had participated in the rodeo. Leeann took pity on them and set about the job herself.

She hadn't finished Sassy before Kristen appeared to help her. "Something's going on," Kristen said, reaching for the saddle on Barbara's pinto pony. "Zach's got Mrs. Childs all riled up, and she's gone to speak to your mother."

"My mother?"

Kristen nodded. "I didn't hear it all but I think they were saying that if you can't stay a while longer, Amos won't let them put the wheelchair-bound kids in the program."

185

A bud of hope sprouted in Leeann. She tried not to let it flower until she had a chance to talk to her mother. That wouldn't be until after the busy dinner hour.

Before Zach left in Kristen's mother's car with Alan, he told Leeann, "Boy, that Mrs. Childs is a tiger. I can see why Amos is scared of her. I pointed her toward your mother, and she charged right into the kitchen like she had a right to be there. Fierce lady. And she looks so sweet."

He shook his head wonderingly as his eyes began to twinkle. "Is that how Joy's going to turn out?"

"I think it's just because Mrs. Childs feels the special-needs kids have to have somebody to fight for them," Leeann said.

"Zach," Kristen called. "We have to go."

"Coming," he said over his shoulder. "Don't forget to let me know what your mother says, Leeann, okay?"

"Okay," she promised.

When everyone had left, Leeann realized how tired she was from the tension of trying to make everything go right at the rodeo. But she went around picking up the trash left near the refreshment table anyway. She'd been too busy to try any of the cookies and punch, or the chips and dip the Childses had brought. Now she was hungry. Suppertime, she thought, and headed toward the ranch house, wondering if Mrs. Childs could have changed Rose's plans for leaving. Leeann doubted

186

it, but then, with Mrs. Childs, anything was possible.

Much later, when she and Rose were alone in their cabin, Leeann asked, "What did Mrs. Childs say to you, Rose?"

"She wants you to stay here another month at least. She even suggested I let you finish out the school year here. It would be her 'pleasure,' she said, to have you stay with Joy and Joey."

"So what did you tell her?"

"Well, I said you and I have never been separated, but I'd think about it."

"So I can't stay?" Leeann asked quietly.

Rose raised her eyebrows. "I don't know, honey. I wasn't enthused about the idea, but Hanna—she was there when Mrs. Childs put in her plea—Hanna pointed out that if I could stand being separated from you for a few weeks, it would be easier for me to find us an apartment and get set with the business."

Rose began undressing to get ready for bed. From the bathroom, she continued, "See, Lydia offered to let me stay with her, but she made it plain she couldn't take us both in. She's fussy about her privacy. Or maybe she thinks a teenage girl would be hard on her antique chairs or something. Anyway, if I lived with her it would save us some money."

Leeann caught her breath. "Then you might let me stay?" she asked.

"Hanna said you could bunk with her." Rose stuck her head out the bathroom door. "She's got a daybed she'd be glad to let you use. And then if you wanted to spend a few weekends with the Childses, that wouldn't be too much to accept from people I barely know. That's if you want to stay, Leeann." Rose was watching for Leeann's reaction.

"Oh, Mama, I do want to stay. Not that I don't want to be with you, but I'm involved in so much going on here right now."

"I don't know how you got so important to the people here so fast," Rose said. "And to Amos of all people!" She laughed.

"I don't know either," Leeann said. "But it feels really good to be needed."

Rose nodded. "I'm glad," she said. "It's nice you found that out about yourself. Just don't forget that I need you, too."

"I won't," Leeann promised.

Impulsively she ran out to the corral and whistled for Sassy. "It's just a temporary reprieve," she told him when he poked his long head over the railing next to hers. She still had to go back to Charlotte eventually. She'd leave Sassy and Zach and Kristen and Joy and the people at Lost River Ranch—but not now, not for a while, not just yet.

She was amazed to find how happy that made her.